Praise for

Lucy Castor Finds Her Sparkle

"A quietly reassuring story showing that change can be a good thing at times." —*Kirkus Reviews*

"This is a feel-good story that draws the reader into the magic and the changes of Lucy's life in a way that is impossible to put downv, the words flowing with an irresistible beauty. This would be a wonderful read-aloud, especially snuggling by a fire on a cold night!" —*School Library Connection*

"[T]his quiet, almost timeless tale may appeal to young readers who are similarly resistant to growing up."

—*School Library Journal*

Also by Natasha Lowe

The Power of Poppy Pendle
The Courage of Cat Campbell
The Marvelous Magic of Miss Mabel

Lucy Castor

Finds Her Sparkle

By NATASHA LOWE

A PAULA WISEMAN BOOK
Simon & Schuster Books for Young Readers
NEW YORK   LONDON   TORONTO   SYDNEY   NEW DELHI

SIMON & SCHUSTER BOOKS FOR YOUNG READERS
An imprint of Simon & Schuster Children's Publishing Division
1230 Avenue of the Americas, New York, New York 10020
This book is a work of fiction. Any references to historical events,
real people, or real places are used fictitiously. Other names, characters, places,
and events are products of the author's imagination, and any resemblance to
actual events or places or persons, living or dead, is entirely coincidental.
Text copyright © 2018 by Natasha Lowe
Cover illustrations copyright © 2018 by Diana Pedott
SIMON & SCHUSTER BOOKS FOR YOUNG READERS
is a trademark of Simon & Schuster, Inc.
For information about special discounts for bulk purchases, please contact Simon
& Schuster Special Sales at 1-866-506-1949 or business@simonandschuster.com.
The Simon & Schuster Speakers Bureau can bring authors to your live event. For
more information or to book an event, contact the Simon & Schuster Speakers
Bureau at 1-866-248-3049 or visit our website at www.simonspeakers.com.
Also available in a Simon & Schuster Books for Young Readers hardcover edition
Book design by Chloë Foglia
The text for this book was set in Garamond 3 LT.
Manufactured in the United States of America
0419 OFF
First Simon & Schuster Books for Young Readers paperback edition May 2019
2 4 6 8 10 9 7 5 3 1
The Library of Congress has cataloged the hardcover edition as follows:
Names: Lowe, Natasha, author.
Title: Lucy Castor finds her sparkle / Natasha Lowe.
Description: First edition. | New York : Simon & Schuster Books for Young
Readers, [2018] | "A Paula Wiseman Book." | Audience: Ages 12 and under.
| Summary: Lucy, nine, does not like change and now, her best friend has
stopped believing in magic and her mother is expecting a baby.
Identifiers: LCCN 2017028134|
ISBN 9781534401969 (hc) | ISBN 9781534401983 (eBook) |
ISBN 97815344-01976 (pbk)
Subjects: | CYAC: Best friends—Fiction. | Friendship—Fiction. | Neighbors—
Fiction. | Pregnancy—Fiction. | Family life—Massachusetts—Fiction. |
Massachusetts—Fiction.
Classification: LCC PZ7.L9627 Luc 2018 | DDC [Fic]—dc23
LC record available at https://lccn.loc.gov/2017028134

For Annabelle and Tris,
who got to share the magic with me!

1

LUCY CASTOR DID NOT LIKE CHANGE. IT MADE her queasy and uncomfortable, and she tried to avoid it at all costs. Luckily, she had lived her whole life in the little western Massachusetts town of Hawthorne, in the same clapboard house on the same street with the same set of parents, so change was not something Lucy had to deal with very often. And when it did come along, she could usually cope with it, like the time her mother decided to make chicken on Monday instead of spaghetti, or insisted Lucy wear a skirt and not her usual sweatpants when they went out for dinner. Or the time her parents replaced their old green sofa (the one Lucy felt certain could fly if she knew the right magic words) without asking her first. These things were mildly upsetting (well, the sofa was heartbreaking) but Lucy generally recovered quite quickly, and life would go on in its familiar, comfortable groove.

At least until the weekend before she entered fourth grade, when a series of monumental events shook Lucy's world, and everything began to change.

2

I T WAS DELICIOUS TO BE HOME, LUCY THOUGHT, standing in the middle of her bedroom. The Castors had been gone all summer, visiting Lucy's grandmother in Vermont, and although this had been absolutely wonderful, there was nothing more exciting than being back in your own house. Especially when you were about to see your best friend, Ella, for the first time in eight weeks.

Wanting to wear her purple shirt with BEST FRIENDS ARE MAGIC written across the front, Lucy skipped over to her closet. She knew it would be in there, because she hadn't taken it to Vermont. The shirt had been a gift from Ella, two years ago on Lucy's seventh birthday. It was definitely on the small side now, but it made Ella smile when Lucy wore it. And something magical always seemed to happen whenever she put it on.

Tugging at the handle of her old pine closet, Lucy could feel the wood had swollen in the humidity. With an extra-hard pull she yanked the door open and gave a gasp of shocked surprise. For an instant Lucy froze, staring inside before quickly slamming the cupboard shut.

Heart pounding, she raced across the hall to her parents' bedroom, where she found her father putting on socks amid a jumble of unpacked suitcases, and her mother still lying in bed. Both these things were highly unusual, because the family had been home for a whole day already, and Mrs. Castor usually unpacked straightaway, plus she always got up early on weekends. But Lucy didn't have time to worry about such matters now. There were far more important things to deal with.

"There's a gnome in my closet," she panted, grabbing her father's hand. "With a long white beard and a red jacket. And he didn't look too happy to see me. He was frowning."

"Probably hanging up your things," Mrs. Castor murmured from the bed.

"No, he wasn't. He was just standing there with his arms folded. Come on, Dad, please hurry," Lucy said, tugging him back to her room. With a grand flourish she opened the closet door, but there was nothing in there except clothes.

Lucy pushed aside the hangers, peering to the back of the cupboard.

"I can't believe it. He's gone. I should have asked him what he was doing. But I was too scared." Lucy gave a shiver.

"I wish I'd seen him," Mr. Castor remarked.

Lucy pointed to her fluffy red sweater hanging at the front of the cupboard. "That was the exact cherry color of his jacket, and he wore these strange gold shoes with toes that curled up at the ends." She closed her eyes, picturing the shoes in her head. "They were more like slippers than shoes, very narrow and sparkly."

"Sounds like a well dressed gnome."

"He was," Lucy said, and then with rising excitement added, "Hey, Dad, look at this." Crouching down Lucy leaned inside the cupboard and touched the floor. She held up her fingers, which had tiny gold sparkles stuck to them. "From his shoes," she whispered, breathing hard.

This was different from the glitter she had used to decorate last year's Christmas presents; the homemade Popsicle stick picture frames she had hidden at the back of her cupboard. That glitter wasn't nearly as sparkly. Lucy was sure of it. She was quite certain. These sparkles were more shimmery, more golden, and she swept some into her hands as evidence.

Scrambling to her feet, Lucy darted over to her bedside

table. She carefully brushed the sparkles into the open drawer, grabbed her special notebook, and sat on the edge of the bed. "I'm going to draw a picture of him, Dad. To show Ella when she comes over." Just the thought of Ella coming over made Lucy start to bounce with happiness. She was aching to see her best friend again. "Joined at the hip," that's what Lucy's dad always said, while Lucy's mom liked to call them "two peas in a pod." They had met on the first day of kindergarten and been inseparable ever since.

"She's going to be so mad she missed seeing him," Lucy said, looking up at her dad, eyes shining. "But she's going to be so excited when I tell her."

Lucy and Ella spent all their free time searching for signs of magic together. They had uncovered tiny (possibly fairy) footprints in the woods near Lucy's house, a bluish speckled stone that had to be a fossilized dragon's egg, and an old key in the garden, which the girls knew unlocked a secret door. They just hadn't managed to find the door yet.

"That's what we're going to do today," Lucy said, drawing a pair of curly-toed shoes on the page. "Go on a gnome hunt. We were going to make magic potions, but this is far more important. We'll search the attic and the basement and then camp out in my cupboard. He's bound to come back."

"I hope so," Mr. Castor said. "But maybe gnomes are scared of humans, Lucy? You could have frightened him away."

"He'll be back," Lucy said with confidence, sketching in the gnome's red jacket.

After eating a bowl of cold cereal Lucy went outside to wait for Ella, taking her notebook and mini binoculars with her. The mini binoculars were perfect for searching out signs of magic as well as spying on the robin's nest in Mrs. Minor's tree next door.

Lucy wanted to locate the magic wands that she and Ella had hidden beneath the rhododendron bush at the end of the yard. Putting her hand under the bush, she felt around and pulled out two sticks decorated with glitter and bits of moss. Each one had a purple ribbon tied around the handle end. Lucy waved her stick (the one with the most glitter) in the air and whispered, "Sparkalicious," which was the magic word she and Ella had invented.

Closing her eyes, Lucy sat very still, the grass soft and warm beneath her. She was sure she could feel magic close by. Probably seeing the gnome this morning had something to do with it, Lucy decided. A bee buzzed softly, and the air smelled faintly of lavender. Lucy breathed deeply and gave a contented smile. This was a perfect "petunia moment."

It had been Lucy's dad who first came up with the idea of petunia moments. Mr. Castor's father, Lucy's grandfather, had been a stickler for time, checking his watch regularly and tapping the glass face when he wanted to hurry everyone up. Lucy's dad said he was so busy worrying about time that he never had any left over to "smell the petunias," which meant noticing all the small, wonderful things that happened in a day, the sort of things you would hurry right by if you weren't paying attention.

A petunia moment could happen anytime, when you suddenly realized that the moment was about as perfect as it could get. Being handed a scoop of your favorite ice cream, for example, or when Lucy was snuggled on the sofa between her parents, listening to her dad read *The Hobbit*. But the petunia moments that Lucy loved the best were the enchanted ones like this, when you knew, with every cell in your body, that magic was definitely nearby. In fact Lucy had a strong suspicion that she herself might actually have magical powers. She was waving her wand in circles when the back door banged open and Ella called out, "Hiya!"

With a loud squeal Lucy scrambled to her feet. "Ella, you're not going to believe this, but I saw a gnome this morning! A real one," Lucy yelled, spinning around. "Ella?" she said again, staring at the girl with the swishy blond ponytail, the short jean shorts, and a cropped white T-shirt with the words SPARKLE GIRL spelled out in pink glitter.

It was definitely Ella, because her face looked the same, and she had on her little gold hoop earrings. But this was not the Ella Lucy knew. That Ella wore crumpled T-shirts and baggy gym shorts, just like Lucy had on now. She wore her hair loose and unbrushed, and she never tilted her head to one side or gave a cute little wave or said "hiya," like this Ella was doing. And never, in a million years, would she have worn a cropped white T-shirt with SPARKLE GIRL printed across the front.

The sparkle girls were part of a hip-hop dance troupe that took lessons at the Sunshine Studio in town. Some of the kids in their class were in it, and last year at recess Molly, Summer, and May used to practice routines, dancing about in their sparkle shirts with their ponytails swishing, while Lucy and Ella mixed up magic potions on the grass, laughing at how the sparkle girls didn't like to get dirty.

Glancing down, Lucy noticed that her legs were streaked with earth, and her BEST FRIENDS T-shirt had a hole under the arm and a faded chocolate stain on the front. She picked bits of grass out of her long brown hair, which she knew was a tangled mess. Normally, none of these things would have bothered Lucy one bit, but standing next to this new glittery Ella made her suddenly self-conscious and shy. Ella's face looked all dewy and fresh, and Lucy couldn't help feeling like a sweaty little mouse with her huge brown eyes and slightly crooked front teeth. Neither of the girls spoke right away, and Lucy rubbed at her shirt with a finger.

"Gosh, I can't believe you can still fit into that," Ella finally said, giving her ponytail a shake. The girls had always been pretty much the same height, but Ella seemed to have grown at least two inches since they last saw each other. Or maybe it was just her high, bouncy ponytail making her appear taller. She glanced at Lucy's magic wand and then looked away, as if she didn't know what it was. An ache lodged in Lucy's chest, and she dropped her wand on the grass. "So how was your summer?" Ella asked with a bright, sparkly smile.

"Good." Lucy nodded, thinking of all the things she had been storing up to tell Ella and how silly they now sounded in her head. Finding a new bird's nest for her collection, trying to come up with a flying spell at her grandmother's house, but most important of all, discovering the gnome in her closet. "When did you become a sparkle girl?" Lucy blurted out, unable to stop herself.

"May wanted me to join the dance troupe. I didn't have much else going on this summer, so"—Ella gave a shrug—"I went along to watch one day, and it's actually really fun." With another swish of her ponytail Ella gave a quick demonstration, performing some fancy hip-hop moves. "You should join too, Lucy. Honestly, I think you'd love it. I never thought I would, but I do."

"I'm not very good at dancing," Lucy said, wondering if Ella was teasing her and this was all a big joke. "I'd hate everyone looking at me."

"There's a show coming up at the end of September," Ella continued, hip-hopping around the yard. "You have to come and watch us. You just have to."

Clearly Ella was not joking, and Lucy swallowed the lump in her throat. She felt as if she had missed an important summer assignment—how to prepare for fourth grade. Obviously, the list included: 1. Become a sparkle girl. 2. Start wearing your hair in a high, bouncy ponytail. 3. Branch out and make lots of new friends who have nothing in common with your old best friend. And number 4, the most upsetting of all—give up caring about magic. Ella hadn't asked one single question about Lucy's gnome since she'd mentioned him, and Lucy could feel her lip trembling.

"Are you all right, Lucy?" Ella asked in concern.

"Just a bit shaken up, that's all," Lucy said, wishing the conversation didn't sound so forced. But she had to tell Ella. It was too important not to, and lowering her voice, Lucy whispered, "I saw a gnome in my closet this morning. At least I think it was a gnome. It could have been an elf or a dwarf." There was a rather long silence, and Lucy added, "I thought we could try and find him." She didn't mention the picture she had drawn.

Ella looked embarrassed. "Come on, Lucy. You don't believe all that stuff anymore."

The ache in Lucy's chest grew sharper. She fiddled with her watch strap and dug her nails into her skin, trying to stop herself from crying. "I found a spectacular nest at my gran's house," she said. "If you want to see it."

"Cool." Ella glanced around as if waiting for someone

else to show up. She started another little series of dance steps, not seeming very interested in Lucy's bird's nest either. "I'm practicing with May and Summer after lunch. You can come too if you want," Ella added. "I'm sure they wouldn't mind."

Lucy's throat grew tight. She had thought Ella was spending the whole day with her, and for a moment she couldn't speak, worried her voice might start to wobble. She wanted so badly to talk with Ella, the old Ella, the one who would have raced upstairs to Lucy's room, wanting to see the sparkles she had found. It felt as if aliens had taken away her best friend and left a strange Ella look-alike in her place.

"Are you all right?" Ella asked, staring at Lucy in concern.

"I've just got a lot to do before school. You know, buy folders and pencils and stuff." Lucy could feel the tips of her ears starting to throb and grow warm the way they always did whenever she was upset, and she gave her hair a shake to cover them.

"I got all my things last week," Ella said. There was a rather long silence between the girls, and Lucy could feel herself getting a headache.

The morning dragged on as Lucy listened to Ella talking about May's swimming pool and how she had been invited to a big Labor Day party there and how Summer had taught her to do backflips off the deep end. Lucy hated to admit it, but she actually felt relieved when Ella finally left. And then she felt sad about being relieved, and even sadder that they hadn't gone up to her room and examined her newest nest together, the one she had found in the woods near her grandmother's house, the one with a crackly piece of snakeskin woven in among the twigs. Her grandmother had told Lucy that some kinds of birds put snakeskin in their nests to scare away flying squirrels, and Lucy had been so excited by this fact she couldn't wait to share it with Ella. But clearly the new "sparkle" Ella wasn't interested in Lucy's nest collection anymore. And she certainly wasn't interested in casting spells or making potions or wanting to search for gnomes.

In fact Lucy wasn't sure if she had anything left in common with her old best friend at all.

3

AFTER ELLA HAD GONE, LUCY SAT ON THE grass, staring at their wands. She couldn't bear to throw them away, but Ella didn't want hers anymore—that much was clear. It was as if the magic had leaked out, and all Lucy could see now were two old sticks covered in glitter and bits of moss. Like a little kid's art project.

Her eyes misted over, and not wanting to think about what had just happened with Ella, Lucy picked up her mini binoculars and aimed them at the maple tree in Mrs. Minor's yard. It had been home that spring to a family of robins, and Lucy and Ella had spent hours watching the birds fly in and out, feeding their babies. But the robins had left right before Lucy went on vacation, and now she desperately wanted the nest for her collection.

Wiping her eyes on her T-shirt, she held the binoculars up again and steadied her gaze. There was definitely a flash of something green, shimmery lime green, woven into the nest, although from this distance it was difficult to tell what it was. Robins used all sorts of strange things for building material, tucking the odd scraps in among the twigs and moss and plant fibers. Lucy had some nests in her room laced with animal fur, string, even bits of newspaper, but nothing decorated with lime green glitter.

She had been planning to take Ella with her to ask Mrs. Minor if she could have the nest. Not that there was much chance she would have said yes, of course, because Mrs. Minor was very possibly a witch. At least that's what the girls had always thought, although Ella probably didn't believe in witches anymore either. Still, regardless of whether her next-door neighbor had a cauldron in her kitchen and flew around Hawthorne on a broomstick at night, she was without question, the grumpiest person Lucy had ever come across. And now she'd never know if Mrs. Minor might have given her the nest, because she wasn't nearly brave enough to go over there by herself and ask.

Giving a sad sigh Lucy twisted the end of the binoculars slightly, bringing the nest into sharper focus. It really was a beauty, but all she could think about was Ella becoming a sparkle girl! Letting the binoculars dangle from her neck, Lucy leapt to her feet and ran over to the split rail fence that divided the Castors' yard from Mrs. Minor's. Under normal circumstances she would never have dared to cross it, but these were not normal circumstances. As far as Lucy was concerned, a tragedy had just occurred.

"I think I've lost my best friend," she whispered mournfully as the need to do something rash and a little bit dangerous overtook her. She would climb up that tree and grab the nest, which would take her mind off Ella and get her exactly what she wanted.

Lucy hoped Mrs. Minor wasn't home. Her car hadn't been parked out front when Lucy said good-bye to Ella, but that didn't make the fear of crossing into a sorcerer's territory any less scary. There might be a hex on the yard, which would keep Lucy captive, so she could never get back out. And Mrs. Minor never went anywhere for very long. Quickly, before she lost her nerve, Lucy jumped over the fence, skirting a pile of cedar boards that hadn't been there when she left for Vermont, and dashed across to the maple tree. With a nervous glance back toward Mrs. Minor's house, Lucy started to climb.

There were plenty of branches to grab on to, and she shimmied right up, pulling herself onto the branch where the bird's nest sat. *Oh, this would be such a perfect spot for a tree house*, Lucy thought, sitting down for a minute to look around. A little wooden house tucked away up here that she could keep her magical treasures in, and for a few brief moments she fantasized that perhaps Mrs. Minor was planning on building one with that big heap of lumber.

But Lucy knew in her heart Mrs. Minor was not the tree house building sort. She was probably planning to put up a shed for her potions and broomsticks, and boring old lawn mower. Mrs. Minor liked to keep her lawn in perfect condition, and the one time Lucy had snuck across it to retrieve a tennis ball, tiptoeing over the green, spongy grass, Mrs. Minor had yelled at her fiercely to get off, and (Lucy was quite certain) thrown an invisible spell in her face.

Looking out from her perch, Lucy took in Mrs. Minor's dark brown house with its small, narrow windows, the blinds pulled most of the way down, and her own little white house that had pale blue shutters and big wooden tubs of petunias in the yard. Beyond that she could see more rooftops, a church spire, and the distant ridge of mountains surrounding Hawthorne. Some of the trees were already starting to turn, and tinges of red and orange dotted the canopy of greens.

Their little town nestled on the Mohawk Trail in the heart of the Pioneer Valley, and (as Lucy's dad informed her) it had been home to the Native Americans long before the first white settlers moved in. Mr. Castor taught history at the local high school, and he was passionate about

Hawthorne's past. So passionate, he even had a collection of arrowheads that he had dug up near the river.

Hawthorne had been attacked many times by different Native American tribes during its early years. Lucy wasn't so keen on the history lessons he liked to give her, but she adored her father's arrowheads. Sometimes she would hold one in her hands and concentrate really hard, hoping she might get transported back to the seventeen hundreds. It hadn't happened yet, but Lucy never stopped believing it could be possible. That is, until now.

Sighing heavily, she heard a door thud, and Chloe, who lived on the other side of the Castors, wandered into her yard. Holding up the binoculars Lucy peered through them, noticing that Chloe had dyed her hair a deep eggplant purple. It had been forest green when Lucy left for her grandmother's. Chloe appeared to be dressed in a tunic thing made out of tinfoil with long silver boots underneath. Lucy knew their weird neighbor had graduated from high school last year, but she had no idea what Chloe was doing now.

The Chloe family, as Lucy called them, had moved in four years ago, and in the beginning Chloe had just been shy—shy and kind of sad-looking, hiding behind her long black hair. Lucy wasn't scared of her then, although the girls rarely spoke. It was only when Chloe started piercing her ears all the way round, chopping off her hair, and wearing black lipstick and too much eye makeup that Lucy began to avoid her.

It was difficult to look away though, and Lucy kept the binoculars focused on Chloe as she began picking leaves off a tree, examining each one carefully before dropping it into a plastic bag. Her mouth moved rapidly, as if she were talking to herself, and her nose ring glistened in the sunlight. Lucy realized that since she'd been away, Chloe had also pierced her eyebrow. Not wanting to be caught spying, she put the binoculars down.

Last year Chloe had come home in a police car, and Lucy still didn't know what she'd done. She wasn't sure she wanted to know either. But at least they didn't yell over there anymore. It had been nice and quiet since Chloe's dad left, and her mom's new boyfriend seemed friendly. He always smiled and said hi to Lucy.

Having no desire for Chloe to discover her in Mrs. Minor's tree, Lucy sat quite still, trying not to rustle. "Please go inside," she whispered, wishing she could make herself invisible. Instead, Chloe walked toward the little dogwood tree that grew near the Castors' fence and began plucking leaves off the spindly branches. Lucy shut her eyes, hoping that the ostrich approach might work, since she didn't know any invisibility spells. If she couldn't see Chloe, then maybe Chloe wouldn't notice her.

Holding her breath, Lucy remained motionless, listening

to the thud of her heart. She sensed, even before daring to look, that Chloe had spotted her. The air suddenly felt all electric and tingly, and, opening her eyes, Lucy gave a soft cry, because Chloe was staring right up at her, the plastic bag clutched in her arms.

"Get down!" Chloe shouted. Lucy started to panic. Maybe Chloe wanted the nest for herself, and reaching along the branch she snatched up the robin's nest. Risking another quick look, Lucy let out a whimper, because Chloe was pointing at Mrs. Minor's house. Was she planning on telling her what Lucy had done? Frantic now, Lucy began to clamber down. She was almost at the ground when a loud knocking cut through the warm afternoon, followed by the scrape of a window being yanked up.

"Get off my property right now," Mrs. Minor yelled, wagging a bony finger at Lucy. That was the witchiest finger Lucy had ever seen, and with a terrified yelp she slipped and lost her footing, falling the rest of the way. Luckily, it wasn't far to the ground, and she landed on the soft grass with just a few minor scrapes to her arm. Scrambling straight up, Lucy started to run, the bird's nest clutched in her hands and the binoculars banging against her chest.

"Private property!" Mrs. Minor shouted again. She slammed down the window as Lucy jumped the little fence, staggering back to the Castors' lawn. She was breathing heavily, and a sick, dizzy sensation forced her to bend over, feeling as if she might be about to faint. Lucy hung like that for a few breaths, staring at her sneakers.

"What on earth were you doing?" Chloe said. It took Lucy a few seconds to realize she was the one being addressed. Straightening up slowly she stared at her purple-haired neighbor. "That woman's a nutcase," Chloe continued. "She hates people going near her yard." Lucy blinked and took a few steps backward. She glanced at her house, getting ready to bolt. "So what were you doing up there?" Chloe asked again.

"Getting this," Lucy said, holding out the nest. "It's for my collection."

"Seriously?" Chloe's purple mouth dropped open in surprise. "You collect bird's nests?"

"This is my nineteenth," Lucy informed her. "And they're all different."

"Unbelievable!" Chloe started to chuckle. "That's insane!"

"No, it's not. And you shouldn't make fun of people's collections." Turning away, Lucy ran across her yard. She pushed open the back door, wondering why they couldn't have nice, normal neighbors like most people.

4

W HAT IS THIS?" LUCY SAID, PEERING INTO
her bowl of tomato soup. "It tastes different from
usual."

"I used milk instead of cream," Mrs. Castor confessed,
leaning against the sink. She was wearing a pair of Lucy's
dad's sweatpants, and her eyes looked all droopy and tired.
"I didn't get to the store yet, Lucy. Dad's gone for me now.
I was hoping you wouldn't notice," she added.

With a worried expression Lucy stared up at her mother.
"I cannot cope with *different* today, Mom. It has not been a
good morning."

"And why is that?" Mrs. Castor said, sitting down at the table opposite Lucy.

"I don't like Chloe. She scares me."

"A lot of teenagers look scary, but that doesn't mean they are. I bet she's very nice underneath all that makeup and green hair."

"It's purple, and I don't think she is," Lucy muttered. "And Ella has changed," she whispered, her mouth quivering at the edges. "I'm not sure we're still best friends." She gave her mother a tragic look. "She's become a sparkle girl, and she's going over to May's this afternoon."

"Ahhh," Mrs. Castor said, her "ahhh" full of understanding. "Well, that is hard. I agree."

A tear dropped into Lucy's soup. "Ella doesn't believe in magic anymore."

"Oh, Lucy," Mrs. Castor murmured, her voice full of sympathy. "It doesn't mean you have to stop."

"But it's hard to believe in magic by yourself," Lucy said. She sniffed and stirred her soup around. "I think that I'd like to be homeschooled this year. You can teach me, Mom. It would be perfect." Lucy's mother wrote for a magazine called *Amazing Animals.* Every month they highlighted a different animal, and it was Mrs. Castor's job to research the animal and write fun facts about it, and since she did all her work on her laptop computer, she could easily teach

Lucy at the same time. "I really don't want to go into fourth grade," Lucy added, needing to make her point.

"Things are never as bad as you imagine they're going to be, Lucy. You know that. And I'd be a terrible teacher, I'm afraid."

"Then Dad can do it. He's a teacher already, so I'm sure we could make it work."

"But he teaches at the high school." Mrs. Castor leaned over to give Lucy a hug. "And he's gone all day."

"Mom, are you all right?" Lucy asked, noticing that her mother's face looked slightly gray and she seemed to be tilting her head away from Lucy's bowl of soup, as if she didn't like the smell.

"If you don't mind, Lucy, I think I shall take a nap. I'm feeling a touch, well, a touch under the weather."

"Aren't you going to make a cake for tea like you always do on Saturdays?" The Castors were big fans of afternoon tea, a tradition Mr. Castor had adopted after a trip to England during his college years.

Mrs. Castor groaned and shook her head. This was not good news at all. After the awful morning she had had, Lucy didn't need any more changes. When Lucy's mother got sick, which was not very often, everything fell apart. They had to have sandwiches for supper, and Lucy's favorite T-shirt didn't get washed, and the house felt all cold and empty.

"Dad will be back soon," Lucy's mother said with a yawn. And she shuffled over to the sofa, clutching Mildred, the blue vomit bucket that came out whenever the Castors were sick. Lucy had christened it Mildred during a violent bout of the stomach flu some years ago, and the name had stuck to the bucket like the faint scent of vomit that never seemed to go away either.

Usually when she had time to herself, Lucy liked to organize her nest collection or make a magic potion or search for secret doorways in the house. She had always believed that behind the stairs or in the attic or the back of a cupboard was a secret passageway leading to a magical world. Perhaps a world where her gnome might have come from? Now though, Lucy didn't feel like searching for gnomes or making a magic potion. Nothing felt the same anymore.

Not wanting to go outside and leave her mother alone in the house, Lucy drifted upstairs to her bedroom. The sparkles in her drawer didn't look quite as sparkly as Lucy remembered, and when she opened her cupboard, it was just an ordinary cupboard, rather messy and full of clothes. She closed her eyes, conjuring up the gnome she was sure she had seen, his curly gold slippers and long white beard and the bright cherry-colored jacket he had worn. But when she opened them, all Lucy saw was her own red sweater hanging at the front of the closet. "I know he was in here," she whispered, needing to convince herself of this. "I know he was." But she didn't want to search without Ella.

Loud screaming cut through the summer afternoon, and Lucy knew, before she even looked out of her window, that it was the O'Brien boys. They lived opposite the Castors, and, glancing across the street, Lucy saw that a large, bright orange plastic car appeared to be the reason for the screaming. Micky, the four-year-old, was attempting to pull two-year-old Billy out of the driver's seat, with Billy still pedaling across the front lawn. Both boys were yelling at full volume, while five-year-old Sammy crouched in a flower bed, dressed in his Batman costume, digging away with what looked like a large kitchen spoon.

Lucy watched Mrs. O'Brien hurry around the side of the house, a wiggling Toady clutched in her arms. Toady was the baby, and even though the family called him that with great affection, Lucy couldn't help feeling rather sorry for the littlest O'Brien, who did indeed look remarkably toad-like with his squashed plump face and kicking legs. He was the only O'Brien child with dark hair. The other three all had Mrs. O'Brien's mess of custard-colored curls, and Lucy found it rather difficult sometimes to tell them apart.

Marching after the car, Mrs. O'Brien swiftly separated the boys, herding them both (and the car) around toward the backyard. Kicking his legs about, Toady joined in the screaming, and Lucy shuddered. She couldn't imagine being part of a big, noisy family like that. Even though it had not been a good day so far, at least she didn't have to live in the O'Brien house. And that was something to be extremely grateful for.

Wishing her dad would hurry up and come home, Lucy drifted back down to the hallway, sitting on the bottom stair to wait. This was one of her favorite places in the house. She found it nice and comforting, listening to the rhythmic ticking of the clocks. Lucy's dad was a big clock collector, as well as a collector of arrowheads. He rescued the clocks from junk shops and flea markets and the local Put and Take, a shed near the railway station where people put things they didn't want that other people could have for free. And on the weekends and in the evenings he liked to take the clocks apart, spreading all the bits over the kitchen table (which drove Lucy's mom a little bit crazy), and fix them up again so that they worked.

There was a loud clang from the kitchen as the station clock struck one. Lucy's father had rescued it from the Hawthorne railway station when they replaced the heavy wooden clock with a new, electric model that didn't require winding. One rainy Sunday Lucy had counted all the clocks in the Castors' house. There were thirty-seven of them sitting on shelves and mantelpieces and hanging on the walls. Thirty-eight if you counted Lucy's old alarm clock.

The clocks didn't all strike the hour, of course, but Lucy, with her eyes closed, could recognize the different chimes of the ones that did. The French porcelain parlor clock had a delicate bell-like tinkle while the banjo clock hanging at the top of the stairs sounded like someone banging a gong. The last clock to strike was always the tall, stately grandfather clock that stood in the Castors' narrow hallway, never seeing any need to rush as it boomed out the hour in a deep, majestic voice.

"Where are you, Dad?" Lucy fretted, winding a strand of hair round and round her finger. How long did it take to go to the store? Her mother had said he'd be back very soon, but that was ages ago, and now Lucy was worried that her father might have been run over by a truck. She was also worried that her mother might be about to die and then maybe she'd have to go and live in the Chloe house next door, or with scary Mrs. Minor, or all those loud O'Briens while her grandmother worked out how she could take care of Lucy full-time. Moving in with Ella's family clearly wasn't an option anymore. She'd be an orphan at nine years old, a small mouselike orphan with ears that stuck out.

When Mr. Castor finally came striding through the door, Lucy hurled herself on him like a stick bug, wrapping her arms around his waist.

"Hey, Lucy Lopkins! It hasn't been that long," Mr. Castor said, managing to put the groceries down with Lucy still attached.

"Something's happened to Ella," Lucy began, launching

right in. "She's not Ella anymore, so I don't have a best friend to start fourth grade with. And Mrs. Minor is evil and should be sent to jail for being a bad neighbor. And I thought you'd been run over by a truck. Oh, and I think Mom might be dying!"

"Gosh! Did I miss all that? Well, I'm okay, so why don't we go check on your mother?"

Mrs. Castor was sprawled across the sofa, snoring softly. "If she doesn't make it, I think we should bury her next to Ginger," Lucy whispered. "That way she'll have company." Ginger was Lucy's guinea pig who had died last year. He was buried in a shoe box under the apple tree.

"Your mother is going to be fine, Lucy. I promise," Mr. Castor said. In her heart Lucy knew this, but she couldn't help the worrying thoughts from taking over her head or the worrying words blurting out of her mouth.

It was a huge relief when Lucy's mom finally woke up from her extremely long middle of the day nap. She certainly wasn't up for cake making, but Lucy and her dad shared a packet of vanilla cookies instead, and they were now all snuggled on the sofa, or "the Nest," as Lucy called it. Whenever they sat here, she always felt like a baby bird, nestled in between her parents, the deep, soft sofa fitting the three of them perfectly.

Things were finally starting to feel normal again (so

long as Lucy didn't think about Ella), with Mr. Castor falling asleep like he usually did in the middle of reading Lucy *The Hobbit*, and Lucy leaning down to draw smiley faces on her dad's ankles. It made her giggle the way his words would get more and more slurred until he started to say the most ridiculous things. Lucy guessed he was almost at the falling asleep properly stage because his head had nodded forward. She could hear her mother's stomach gurgling. It was all extremely peaceful, just the three of them sitting there, and Lucy realized that together they added up to a prime number.

Her grandmother was a math professor, and she had been teaching Lucy about prime numbers this summer. Lucy's gran got more excited over math than anyone else Lucy knew. But her gran was right, Lucy mused as she snuggled between her parents. Prime numbers were pretty special. They couldn't be divided by anything other than one and themselves, and she decided right then, that three was her favorite prime number of all. Lots of wonderful things came in threes. Wishes from a magic lamp, three little pigs, three billy goats gruff. Just like her mom, her dad, and herself. They made a perfect threesome. Even with Ella finding new friends to hang out with and giving up magic, and Mrs. Minor yelling, nothing could divide the Castors.

Lucy would have been happy to stay nesting on the sofa

all evening, but Mr. Castor woke up and said they should think about supper, and Mrs. Castor thought she might be able to manage a little chicken soup. So Lucy's dad heated up some from a can, while Lucy laid the table, putting down three spoons and three bowls in a perfect circle (like the three bears eating their porridge).

"I have important news," Lucy informed her parents, buttering a piece of bread. "I have just decided that three is my favorite number in the whole world. It's a prime number, you see, and I'm extremely fond of it. So if you'd ever like to buy me an unbirthday present, I'd love a T-shirt with the number three on the front." Glancing down at her purple shirt Lucy said sadly, "This one doesn't fit anymore."

"We can definitely buy you a new shirt," Mr. Castor replied, spooning up soup. "But I, um, I've always thought that four was a rather nice number myself. It's balanced. Two on this side, two on that side."

"Two is not a good number," Lucy said sadly, thinking about her un–best friend, Ella.

"Oh, I agree with your dad. Four is marvelous," Mrs. Castor said, stirring her soup around but not actually trying any. "Lots of things come in fours," she added. "Fancy cupcakes, bottles of cream soda, packs of socks."

"There is nothing special about four." Lucy shuddered. "It is ugly and common and completely unmagical. I much prefer three."

Mrs. Castor glanced at her husband, and he gave a little nod. "We have important news too, Lucy," Mrs. Castor said, pushing her bowl of soup away. She paused for a moment and pressed a handkerchief against her mouth as if she might be sick again.

"Oh, you are dying," Lucy wailed. "I guessed it earlier, and you didn't know how to tell me. You knew I was sad about Ella, and you didn't want to add to my worries. You've got some terrible illness, haven't you? That's why you keep being sick and you look all gray and old."

"Lucy, this is good news," Mrs. Castor said, glancing at her husband again. Her voice was soft and quivery. "We're going to have a baby."

Lucy sat quite still, listening to the station clock ticking away as she tried to absorb her mother's words. She should be happy. She knew she should. Wasn't that how you were meant to feel when your parents announced you were going to be a big sister? Summer had danced around the classroom in second grade, saying she couldn't wait to babysit her new little brother, talking about all the things they would do together. But Lucy was nine years old. She had been an only child her whole life, and why on earth would her parents want another baby now?

These are the things Lucy knew she should say: *I'm so happy, Mom and Dad. This is the best news ever. Having a baby will make our family complete. I can't wait to be a big sister.*

These are the things Lucy wanted to say: *This will ruin my whole, entire life. How could you do this to me? Aren't I enough? You're far too old to have a baby. Babies cry and scream and smell, and why would anybody want one? We'll turn into a loud family like the O'Briens, and our baby will look like a toad. I can't even talk to my best friend about this, because she's not my best friend anymore. I hate, hate, hate the number four.*

The station clock struck six, and Lucy's parents were still waiting for her to say something. They had moved close together and were holding hands, and for the first time in her life Lucy felt completely left out.

She tried to say *How wonderful*, but her mouth refused to cooperate.

"This is not a petunia moment," Lucy finally whispered, wishing she could turn the clocks back and start a different weekend all over again.

5

AFTER DINNER LUCY RAN STRAIGHT TO HER room, too upset to play crazy eights or watch a movie, both of which Mr. Castor had suggested. If only she could call Ella to talk about the baby. Ella would understand how she felt. But Ella hadn't understood about the gnome, and she was probably having a sleepover at Summer's house, which made Lucy feel even more alone.

She could hear loud bursts of laughter coming from outside, and peering through the window Lucy saw Chloe standing on the sidewalk, talking to her two weird friends, a boy with hedgehog spiked hair and a girl dressed all in black, long dark hair hanging almost to her waist. They looked just as intimidating as Chloe, and Lucy quickly stepped back so they wouldn't see her.

Turning away she picked up her new robin's nest from one of the long shelves that Mr. Castor had built especially for her collection. Nests were strangely comforting, Lucy thought, like little homes that could protect you from the world, and this was definitely one of her fanciest additions. The lime green glittery things turned out to be little bits of ribbon, green shimmery ribbon with a thin silver stripe running through them, woven right into the nest. And lining the middle of the nest were soft strands of green and orange hair that looked remarkably like some of Chloe's. She had gone through an orange phase early in the spring before dyeing her hair forest green. Brushing a stray twig off the shelf, Lucy put the nest back down and walked over to her bureau mirror.

Sometimes when she studied her face, Lucy saw a pretty elf princess with sticky out elfin ears poking through her long brown hair, or, depending on her mood, a small frightened mouse with enormous mouse ears and huge brown worried mouse eyes. This was definitely a mouse evening. In fact it was such a mouse evening Lucy wouldn't have been at all surprised if she'd gone and sprouted a tail.

Of course her parents wanted another baby, Lucy thought. One that didn't look like a rodent. Opening the top drawer of her bureau, she took out the enormous roll of extra-wide sticky tape she kept in there. Pulling off a long sticky strip, Lucy taped her ears close to her head. That's how she went to sleep on bad ear days, hoping they would be lying flat when she woke up. This hadn't happened yet though. It just made a terrible tangle of her hair.

But, luckily, if Lucy went to bed as a mouse, she would usually wake up as an elf princess. Her mouse moods never lasted long. Although Lucy had a horrible feeling that she might not feel like an elf princess again for a long, long time. And not just because of the baby news either. Pretending to be an elf princess in fourth grade suddenly seemed babyish and silly. Just like believing in magic.

Jumping into bed, she buried herself under the covers, making a cozy mouse nest big enough for precisely one. One was also a prime number. It didn't need anybody else. It was all by itself, and as Lucy lay curled up in a ball, she decided that one was now, without question, her new favorite number.

"Lucy, can we come in?" Mrs. Castor called out, knocking on the door.

"I'd rather you didn't," Lucy called back. "I'm not in a talking sort of mood right now."

"Sweetheart, you don't need to talk. You can just listen," Mrs. Castor said, and Lucy heard her bedroom door creak open. Then she felt two hippopotamuses settle on her bed, squashing half her mouse nest.

Mr. Castor cleared his throat. "I know this is going to be a big change," he began.

"And we know how you feel about change," Mrs. Castor added, patting Lucy's bottom.

"But it won't alter how much we love you," they both said together.

Lucy poked her head out of the covers. "I thought we made big decisions together," she said, her mouse fur bristling. "And nobody asked me how I felt about having another baby."

"Well, it wasn't exactly planned," Mrs. Castor confessed. "We were told we wouldn't be able to have any more children, or that it wasn't very likely."

"So this," Mr. Castor said, "was something of a surprise. For all of us."

"A nice surprise," Mrs. Castor added.

"Mmm," Lucy murmured, taking great interest in the opposite corner of the room.

"Lucy, both your dad and I are only children," Mrs. Castor said. "We grew up without brothers or sisters, and it was lonely."

"It was," Mr. Castor agreed.

"But I'm not lonely at all. I'm quite fine," Lucy reassured them. "That is not something you need to worry about."

"We always hoped we'd be able to give you a sibling," Mrs. Castor went on. "You'll make a wonderful big sister, Lucy. This baby is going to be so lucky."

"And where is it going to sleep?" Lucy asked. "Has anybody thought of that? There's no room in this house for a baby."

"In the beginning it will sleep in our room," Mrs. Castor said. "And then when he or she is older, well, we thought it might be nice if you both shared a room."

"Did you?" Lucy said, tipping her head to one side as she pondered this idea. "How about the attic?" she suggested. "We could put it in there."

"Lucy, it's going to be all right, I promise," Mrs. Castor said, leaning toward her daughter for a good-night kiss.

Before the kiss made contact, Lucy scuttled away. "I'm sorry," she announced rather sadly, "but I really don't feel in a kissing sort of mood right now either. This is not turning out to be a good weekend."

"Get some sleep, Lucy," Mr. Castor suggested. "Things will seem brighter in the morning."

"Tomorrow is Sunday, and you will still be having a baby. And the day after that I have to start fourth grade without a best friend," Lucy said. "I see no brightness on the horizon." She gave a sad little sniff. "I wish I was still back at Gran's house."

"Night, night, Lucy Lopkins," her dad said, giving her his crooked smile. "All will be well."

All would not be well, Lucy worried, staring at her mother's stomach. And who would she eat lunch with at school now and play with at recess and partner up with for science projects?

"Sleep tight, Lucy Lopkins," her mother added.

Lucy dived back under the covers. "Please don't call me that anymore," she snapped in a muffled voice. "My name is Lucy."

"Good night, Lucy," Mr. and Mrs. Castor said together, getting up off the bed. Lucy heard them walk across the room and the door creak open. She wanted to call them back, to tell them it was okay, that they could call her Lucy Lopkins if they wanted to, just not in public or when she had friends over. But her throat was all choked up with angry feelings and she couldn't get any words out.

After they had left, even though she was about to go into fourth grade, Lucy rooted around under her bed for her stuffed blue mouse and gave his furry nose a kiss. He smelled deliciously unwashed and familiar and thankfully hadn't changed one bit.

6

LUCY WOKE EARLY TO THE SOUND OF BANG-ing. It was coming from the direction of Mrs. Minor's property, and with a dramatic sigh Lucy got out of bed and pulled open the curtains. There was a truck parked in front of Mrs. Minor's house, but the noise clearly seemed to be coming from around the back. Hurrying across the landing and into the bathroom Lucy peered through the window overlooking the yard. And it was worse than she could possibly have imagined, far worse than a lawn mower shed. "How dare she!" Lucy cried out, spinning on her heels and marching straight down to the kitchen.

"Emergency!" Lucy exploded. "Have you seen what Mrs.

Minor is doing?" Lucy's mother, still in her dressing gown, was slumped across the round oak table, while her father stood at the stove making French toast. "My whole life is falling apart," Lucy wailed. "What else can go wrong?"

"You mean the new fence?" Mr. Castor said, far too calmly for Lucy's liking.

"That is not a fence," Lucy declared, pointing at the kitchen window. "It's going to be a prison wall, a zoo enclosure, a, a sun blocker-outer." Between the Castors' yard and Mrs. Minor's, three workmen were hammering the tall boards together. They had pulled up the little split rail fence that used to divide the properties, and hefty new support posts now stood in place.

"It will block out all our sun," Lucy fumed, marching right over to the window and giving the builders her maddest stare, even though they weren't looking. "We'll have to live in shadow for the rest of our lives. I'll get rickets and stop growing. That's what happens when you don't get enough sunlight, you know. Your body can't absorb vitamin D and your bones go all bendy." Lucy had been reading up on rickets at the doctor's office. They had a lovely illustrated book in the waiting room, all about growing up in the nineteenth century when children worked in mines and factories and suffered from things like scarlet fever, smallpox, and rickets.

"That's a touch dramatic, Lucy," Mrs. Castor murmured,

looking slightly green. "Although I do have to agree. I'm not sure what was wrong with the old fence."

"She obviously wants more privacy," Mr. Castor pointed out. "Something you can't see over."

"So let's go and talk to her about it," Lucy said. "Ask her to take it down. Maybe she could give it to the O'Briens. They're the ones that need a fence to stop all those boys from escaping."

"She's not the easiest person to talk to," Mr. Castor remarked. "Don't forget we have tried. She's never come to one of our picnics."

"She's mean," Lucy added. "She probably wants that wall there so we can't see her making all her evil spells."

"Eat some breakfast, Lucy, and then we'll deal with the fence," Mr. Castor said, flipping over French toast.

"I can't." Lucy shook her head violently. "I feel extremely sick and I think I might die from the shock. So if that happens, please bury me next to Ginger."

Mr. Castor ate a great deal of French toast slathered in local maple syrup, because he didn't want to waste it, while Lucy stared out of the window with an agonized expression on her face, and Mrs. Castor nibbled on a cracker.

By the time they walked outside, a quarter of the fence was already up, and Lucy groaned in dismay. Chloe was watching the progress from her yard. She had her arms folded across a denim jacket studded with rhinestones and looked about as mad as Lucy felt. Her eyes were outlined with heavy black makeup, and she reminded Lucy of an angry panda. "I really hoped she was going to build a nice deck or something," Chloe exclaimed. "I honestly never thought she'd do that."

"I know," Lucy agreed, walking over. "It's going to be so ugly."

"And tall," Chloe added.

"She didn't even ask," Lucy said, surprised that she was having a proper conversation with Chloe. Although it wasn't really that surprising, Lucy realized. Disasters were meant to bring people together, and this was definitely a disaster. Like the time everyone on Lucy's street lost power except for the Schniders, who invited the whole street over for a potluck supper until the electricity came back on again.

"She's stealing all our sun," Lucy fumed. "You would think she would have asked us first."

"My friend Jack says she's a recluse."

"What's a recluse?"

"Someone who doesn't like being around people."

"Just yelling at them," Lucy said. "She likes that."

"I don't think she wants to be able to see your house," Chloe commented.

"Why? Our house is lovely." Lucy turned to look at the rose bushes blooming in one corner of their yard, the straggly apple tree, and the overflowing tubs of petunias. Okay, so the window frames needed painting and some of the shingles had fallen off the roof, the grass could do with a trim and a couple of the paving stones around the house were cracked, but it was absolutely, without question, the most beautiful home in the world, and Mrs. Minor not wanting to look at it sent a sharp pain through Lucy's heart.

"I'm going inside," Chloe said. "I can't bear to watch." Jamming her hands in her pockets, she took a few steps toward her house and then spun back around to face Lucy. "Hey, you know I wasn't making fun of your nest collection yesterday," Chloe called out.

"Well, why did you laugh then and call it insane?" Lucy asked in a slightly wounded voice.

"Because it's quirky," Chloe replied. "Quirky but kind of cool. And I like that!"

"You do?"

"I do." Chloe nodded, walking back off.

"I'm going to get her to take that fence down," Lucy shouted after Chloe, suddenly feeling brave. Chloe didn't turn around. She just raised her arm in salute and kept on walking.

Lucy raced over to her parents, who were standing beside the new fence. "I've just been talking to Chloe, and I think you're right, Mom," Lucy panted. "She isn't nearly as scary as I thought. And she hates this horrible fence as much as we do." Turning to the builders, Lucy pressed her hands together and said, "Could we speak to Mrs. Minor about this, please? I just can't bear it. I'm sure she'll change her mind when I explain how sad this is making me, and Chloe."

"We're not to interrupt her unless it's an emergency," one of the workmen said, holding up a board.

"This is an emergency," Lucy insisted.

"Come on, Lucy, it's not that bad," Mrs. Castor said, putting an arm around her daughter.

"Let's just take it down ourselves," Lucy said fiercely. "It's as much our fence as it is hers."

"No, I'm afraid it's not." Mr. Castor sighed. "She put it up on her land, so there's nothing we can do."

"Except make the best of it," Mrs. Castor said, looking as if she might be about to throw up in the petunias. "Oh, Lucy, it could be worse. It could be twice as tall and block all the sun from the bedrooms, too."

The Castors were excellent at "making the best of it," and they all stood in silence for a while, trying to come up with some "making the best of it" suggestions.

"We won't get too hot out here on sunny afternoons," Mr. Castor eventually said. "It will be nice to have a shady side to the yard, and we won't need the sun umbrella when we have cookouts now."

"Yes, and we can plant some different kinds of flowers,"

Mrs. Castor added. "Ones that like lots of shade."

They both looked at Lucy, waiting for her suggestion. What Lucy wanted to say was, *I hate it. It's like being in jail when you stand on that side of the yard. I'm going to get rickets. All our flowers near the fence will die, and I wish Mrs. Minor would move to Africa and get eaten by a lion. I also wish you weren't having a baby and Ella hadn't become a sparkle girl, and I really, really wish I could see my gnome again.* Instead, what she did say was, "I guess I can practice handstands against the fence. That should be quite fun."

Lucy tried for a smile, but her lips felt all stiff and unbendy. She wished the sun would come out, because that always made everything feel more cheerful. And then Lucy realized that the sun was out. It just didn't shine where she was standing anymore.

7

WHY DON'T YOU CALL ELLA?" MRS. CASTOR suggested later on that morning. "See if she wants to come over and play." Lucy had been sitting at the kitchen table for almost an hour, staring out of the window, while her mother lay on the couch with Mildred, the vomit bucket, beside her. "You can't spend the whole day watching them put up that fence."

"I don't think Ella is interested in playing with me anymore," Lucy said, sighing.

"Well, it's worth a try," Lucy's dad said. He was fiddling about inside the back of a clock with a screwdriver. "Maybe you just got the wrong impression yesterday.

And Ella always comes over on Sundays."

"I don't know." Lucy worried, but she picked up the phone and dialed Ella's number, because it did seem odd not having a playdate on Sunday. When she put the phone down, her lip was quivering, and Lucy's dad gave her a sympathetic look.

"Not going to work?" Mr. Castor said.

"She wasn't there. I talked to her mom. She's hanging out with Summer today." Lucy sniffed and wiped her nose with the back of her hand. "I don't think Ella has playdates anymore. She's a hanger outer now."

"Well, you'll see her at school tomorrow," Mrs. Castor said. "I'm sure everything will be back to normal by then." But Lucy wasn't sure about this at all.

Lucy spent the rest of the day wandering around the house, looking for secret doorways in the backs of all the closets, but it wasn't the same without Ella. She sat cross-legged in her closet, trying to conjure up her gnome again. She sat very still with her eyes closed, breathing quietly so she wouldn't frighten him off. But however hard she concentrated, she couldn't bring back that magical feeling from yesterday, the feeling that anything was possible. It was as if Ella had taken the magic with her when she left, and all Lucy felt was empty.

By the time Monday morning arrived, Lucy was so anxious about school that her stomach felt as if a pit of snakes had moved in. When she looked in the mirror, she was still most definitely a mouse, and Lucy wondered if she should try wearing a ponytail like Ella and the other sparkle girls. Maybe that would make her feel more bouncy. Brushing her hair away from her face, Lucy gathered it up and stared at her reflection. She gave a squeal of horror. Her ears stuck out like curly cabbage leaves, and she quickly let go, smoothing her brown hair back into place.

"Where's Mom?" Lucy asked, trudging into the kitchen. It was amazing how different the room felt without the early morning sunshine streaming in, and Lucy glared at Mrs. Minor's horrible fence.

"Mornings are her worst time," Mr. Castor said. "So I told her to stay in bed. She can work on kangaroos up there." Lucy's mom was researching kangaroos for an upcoming edition of *Amazing Animals*.

"Mornings are my worst time," Lucy said, "especially first day of school mornings. Perhaps I should go back to bed too?"

"How about some cereal?"

"How about a nice plate of bacon and sausage and eggs?"

"It's a school morning for both of us, Lucy, and I'm in charge of breakfast, so cereal or toast, I'm afraid."

"Mom would have made me pancakes, or muffins, or

waffles. Especially on the first day of school."

"Sorry, Lucy. This is a bit of a change for all of us, I'm afraid." Lucy noticed that her father's shirt was crumpled, and he had dripped coffee down his trousers.

"That's all right," Lucy reassured him. "I don't think I could manage bacon and eggs anyway. I may not be having a baby, but I do have a sore tummy. In fact I probably shouldn't go to school, because it really is quite painful, and it might be an inflamed appendix. If those burst, it's very dangerous." Lucy had read all about appendicitis at the doctor's office, along with the perils of rickets.

"You can call me if it gets worse," Mr. Castor said firmly. "I'll come and pick you right up."

"Well, let's just hope it's not too late," Lucy replied. "How would you feel if I died in gym class?"

Usually Lucy's mom took her to school, but sometimes, toward the end of last year, Lucy had met up with Ella and the two of them would walk together. It wasn't far, and Hawthorne was as safe a little town as you could get. Today though, since Ella hadn't called to arrange this, Lucy's dad dropped her off on his way to the high school, which made everything feel upside down and strange. Even with her new backpack and pencil box Lucy still felt unprepared, as if she were missing something extremely important and couldn't remember what it might be.

Her dad leaned over and gave her a quick hug. Thankfully, nobody seemed to be watching. "You're going to have a great day, Lucy Lopkins. I mean Lucy, just Lucy," Mr. Castor added quickly.

"Do you think Mom will have made a cake for tea?" Lucy said. "Because that would be something nice to look forward to."

"I wouldn't expect one," Mr. Castor replied. "I think the next few weeks are going to be a bit tough for your mother." Lucy nodded, staring out of the car window. She had a strong feeling the next few weeks, or months, or possibly the rest of her life, judging by the look of things, were going to be pretty tough for her, too.

Opening the car door, Lucy slowly gathered her stuff. She could see Ella on the playground, standing beside Summer and May and Molly. They were all wearing capri style jeans with long sleeved scoop neck shirts. This must have been decided on in advance, Lucy thought, and she couldn't help feeling left out. Why hadn't Ella told her, and why on earth had she worn sweatpants and her favorite, old, soft as butter T-shirt? Clearly this was not the dress code for fourth grade, and Lucy looked around the crowded playground, not knowing who to stand with.

"Hey, Lucy," Ella called, waving to her.

"Oh, hi," Lucy called back in relief, hurrying over to the group. They were talking about something funny that had happened at their last dance rehearsal. Molly kept bursting into giggles and saying "I was so embarrassed!" over and over again, while the other girls kept patting her on the shoulder and saying "It wasn't that bad, Molly. It really wasn't." Lucy had no idea what the girls were talking about, and since no one bothered to tell her, she just stood next to Ella, shuffling her feet and feeling uncomfortable.

When the bell went for class, Lucy followed the girls in to the fourth-grade room. They perched on one of the windowsills, swinging their legs and waiting for Ms. Fisher, their teacher. There wasn't space for a fifth person, so Lucy headed for a desk, stumbling over Rachel Williams's ancient accordion case that took up most of the aisle. Rachel had joined the school last year in the middle of third grade, becoming the only accordion player in Hawthorne Elementary. This was probably a good thing, Lucy felt, judging from the sounds Rachel's instrument had made.

"Sorry," Lucy apologized, scuffing the case with her shoe. It took Rachel, buried in a book as usual, a moment to look up, and she gave a dazed smile, as if she had been somewhere far away. Lucy wished she were far away too, back home in her safe cozy bedroom. Sitting down at an empty desk, she glanced back at the windowsill, hoping Ella would come and sit beside her.

Much to Lucy's relief Ella did, and in between math and science Ella had smiled at Lucy and asked her what she thought of Ms. Fisher. "She seems nice, but a bit strict," Lucy said, hoping this might be the start of a proper conversation. She was desperate to tell Ella about her baby news. Ella would understand. Ella always understood. But then Ella had turned to Summer, who was asking her if she wanted to come over to her house before dance class this evening. And Lucy was left looking at the back of Ella's ponytail.

Recess was even worse. Lucy wandered around feeling like a lost puppy. She stood by, watching the sparkle girls practice their moves for a bit, and then drifted over to the swings, but the swing girls didn't seem to notice she wanted to join in, so after a few minutes Lucy left there, too. Rachel was sitting under the big maple tree, reading. It was clearly a funny book because she gave a snort of laughter and pushed her glasses back up her nose. She didn't seem to mind being alone, and Lucy didn't want to disturb her. The usual group of boys was playing soccer, and as Lucy walked by she got in the way of Jarmal Johnson's kick and felt the ball smack her right in the back.

"Sorry, Lucy," Jarmal called. "Are you all right?"

"I'm fine." Lucy nodded, blinking back tears. She would not cry in front of the whole fourth grade. She would not.

When the bell finally rang at the end of the day, Lucy

saw Ella head off with Molly and Summer. She did wave to Lucy and call out "Bye," but the girls had their arms linked together, and Lucy wasn't so sure how she felt about one being the best prime number anymore. Right now one felt extremely lonely.

8

ON HER WAY HOME FROM SCHOOL LUCY stopped in at the Put and Take. Over the years she had found some of her best treasures here. The Put and Take was a great way of recycling and had earned the town a green star by a local environmental group. The Castors had acquired many useful and not so useful things, including old clocks, a Crock-Pot, and stacks of used books. In second grade Lucy had discovered an oil lamp she was quite sure had a genie inside, and last year she brought home a rather moth-eaten carpet, hoping it might be able to fly, and an old book called *Nature's Magic* that she was positive had belonged to a witch. It was full of recipes and remedies using ingredients you might find in the woods, and the handwritten notes in the margin were scrawled in purple ink. Lucy still felt that somewhere, hidden in the pages, were real spells for invisibility potions or stopping time. She just hadn't found them yet.

So far none of these things had quite lived up to its potential, but Lucy never stopped believing that someday she would unearth something truly magical. Pushing open the door of the Put and Take, she stood quite still for a moment, a little shiver of hopefulness running through her. Lucy saw a chipped, gilt framed mirror, which hadn't been there on her last visit, lying on the table in the center of the room. Holding her breath she peered over the speckled glass, hoping to see swirls of smoke that might clear and show her where her gnome was hiding. But all she saw was her own freckled face and a pair of rather large ears poking through her uncombed hair.

Lucy reached out a hand, and concentrating hard she touched the glass, wanting to feel it go all wobbly, like water, so she could dive through to another world. But instead of swirly liquid beneath her fingertips, all Lucy felt was the smooth, cold surface of the mirror. Smothering a disappointed sigh, she trudged back out, feeling angry at Ella, as if she were somehow responsible for sucking all the magic out of the Put and Take.

As Lucy passed the O'Briens' house, a black stuffed bat

came flying across the lawn and hit her on the nose. Luckily, it was soft and velvety and didn't hurt, but it still made her eyes water.

"Sorry," Sammy yelled, racing after the bat. "NO, don't touch," he screamed as Lucy bent to pick up the toy animal. "He's got evil superpowers. You'll turn into green goo if you touch him."

"You're touching him," Lucy said as Sammy grabbed the bat by a wing and hurled him back toward the house.

Mrs. O'Brien poked her head around the door; a wiggling Toady balanced on her hip. Lucy watched Billy waddle outside, wearing nothing but a very full, by the look of it, diaper, chewing on the corner of the little cardboard book he always carried around with him. "Sammy, no going into the front yard by yourself, please," Mrs. O'Brien called out. "And, Billy, upstairs now to get changed. Oh, hi, Lucy," she added with a smile.

"Hi," Lucy called back.

"Hi," Billy copied, pulling the book out of his mouth and waving it in her direction.

"I won't turn into green goo because I'm a superhero. You're not," Sammy said, trampling over Lucy's foot and charging toward his mother.

"How was school?" Mrs. Castor called out, hearing Lucy come in. She was lying on the sofa with her computer open on her stomach but didn't appear to be writing anything. Mildred sat beside her, and the breakfast dishes were still on the table.

"I don't think I'll be going back," Lucy said, helping herself to the remains of the vanilla finger cookies.

"Oh, Lucy, I'm sure it will get better," Mrs. Castor said. "Would it help if I signed you up for hip-hop lessons with Ella too?"

"No, they would all laugh at me. And I don't want to be a sparkle girl. Perhaps we could read some *Hobbit?*" Lucy suggested. "Dad wouldn't mind if we read ahead, and that would help me forget my worst day of school ever. Which," Lucy finished up, "ended with Sammy O'Brien throwing an evil bat in my face."

"Not on purpose, I'm sure."

"Doesn't matter. It's just lucky I didn't need stitches," Lucy replied. "And I'll probably have terrible bruises tomorrow. *The Hobbit* would take my mind off the pain."

"Oh, Lucy, I'm sorry, but reading makes my nausea worse. It's hard enough staring at this computer." Mrs. Castor closed her eyes as if she'd had a really busy, racing around sort of day and was exhausted. "Did you know that when a baby kangaroo is born it's the size of a jelly bean?"

"I did know that," Lucy said, sighing. "I read about it in my *Book of Strange Facts.*"

"I think I'll take a little nap," Mrs. Castor murmured.

"I can't stare at a screen any longer." Lucy thought about climbing on to the sofa too, but there wasn't room, so she took her cookies out into the yard.

Since there was sun on only one side in the afternoon now, Lucy pulled a garden chair over to the sunny half and propped her feet up on the split rail fence that divided their yard from Chloe's. She couldn't bear to look at Mrs. Minor's fence, so she sat with her back to it. The tree Chloe had been picking leaves from on Saturday was already turning a rusty red color, and Lucy decided that September was not a happy month. Things started to die and change was everywhere.

It was too late to escape when Chloe walked into her yard, carrying a book. She was wearing a long floaty green dress, covered in leaves. They fluttered as she moved, and Lucy couldn't help staring.

"What are you looking at?" Chloe said, fiddling with one of the many rings in her ear.

"Your dress," Lucy admitted. She had never met anyone as direct as Chloe before. "It's the sort of thing an elf princess would wear. But I love it," Lucy added, to show that this was a compliment and not an insult.

"Do you? Really?" Chloe said. Lucy gave an enthusiastic nod. And then something surprising happened. Chloe smiled. It was a slow, spreading smile that transformed her whole face, as if a light had been switched on inside. "It's my own design. I made it."

"Wow!" Lucy looked impressed. "How do you make a dress?"

"I sketched it out, then I bought the fabric and sewed it. The leaves aren't real, of course. They're satin, but I traced them using real leaves from our tree, so each one's a bit different. And I cut up all this ribbon to make a fringe." Chloe twirled around so the strips of sparkly green ribbon caught the sunlight.

"Oh! Oh!" Lucy gasped, pressing her hands to her cheeks. "Don't go anywhere, Chloe. I'll be right back." She sprung up from her chair, unable to contain her excitement. "I have something amazing to show you," Lucy shouted as she ran toward her house. She sprinted straight upstairs to her bedroom, picked up the robin's nest, and ran back out to the garden.

"Look at this," Lucy yelled, rushing back to Chloe, who had settled herself cross-legged on the grass. She handed the nest over the fence, pointing at the bits of lime green ribbon. "It's some of your fringe—see!"

"So it is," Chloe marveled, turning the nest around. "Same silver stripe and everything." She looked up at Lucy and grinned. "I bet the robins found these in my yard. I often sit out here, and I'm always leaving my scraps lying about."

"And inside, look. It's your hair. No one else has hair those colors."

"This is the coolest thing!"

"Some birds will use anything when they build their nests," Lucy said, feeling a sudden wave of panic in case Chloe had thought the nest was a gift. She held out her hands, but Chloe didn't notice.

"Gosh, this is woven so tightly, almost like a piece of fabric. It's magic the way birds can do this."

"Yes, it is," Lucy said, waggling her fingers and clearing her throat.

"Oh, sorry, I'm taking too long, aren't I?" Chloe leaned forward and gave the nest back. Then she picked up her book and showed Lucy the cover. It was The *Lord of the Rings*, written by the same person who had written *The Hobbit*. "Lady Arwen is my inspiration for this whole line of clothes I'm designing. She's an elf princess in *The Lord of the Rings*."

"I had no idea you were so clever," Lucy said, and Chloe burst out laughing.

"You thought I was a high school loser, right?"

Lucy's ears flamed with heat. "I didn't mean it like that."

"It's all right, Lucy. I know what you meant." Chloe smiled to show she wasn't annoyed and smoothed out some of the leaves on her dress. "That's what I want to be though, a fashion designer." She crossed her glittery green nails. "I've applied to Prachets Design College. It's in Boston."

"Well, I'm sure you'll get in," Lucy said, thinking that maybe it was all right to like elf princesses in fourth grade after all. And if it was okay to like elf princesses, then maybe it was okay to believe in magic.

"Thanks." Chloe tucked some bits of floppy purple hair back behind her ears and started to read.

Before she could stop herself, Lucy blurted out, "Do you believe in magic, Chloe?" regretting the words as soon as they had left her mouth. Chloe would think she was silly and childish, and Lucy looked away, cringing as she heard Chloe laugh.

"Of course I believe in magic. Don't you?"

Turning back, Lucy saw that she was smiling again. But it was a nice smile, not a "making fun of Lucy" smile. "I do." Lucy nodded and then said, "My friend Ella doesn't. She used to, but she gave it up over the summer."

"That's too bad. Especially when there's so much magic in the world. It's everywhere," Chloe said. "Magical things happen all the time. You just have to know where to look."

Lucy stared hard at Chloe's face. "Do you really believe that, Chloe?"

"Course I do." She pointed at Lucy's nest. "That's a piece of magic right there. And whenever I come up with a new design, I get all tingly and excited." Chloe looked down at her dress and touched one of the leaves. "This idea just floated into my head."

"Like magic," Lucy whispered.

"Exactly. And the way my mom met her boyfriend,

right after saying how nice it would be to have someone to go to the movies with again. She bumped into him outside Valley Donuts that very afternoon. They were both eating honey glazed crullers, and they both love sappy romantic comedies. Now, don't tell me that wasn't magic."

"What about gnomes?" Lucy asked rather breathlessly. "Do you believe in those, Chloe? Because I think I saw one in my closet."

"A gnome?"

"Well, he could have been an elf or a dwarf. I don't really know. He was wearing a red jacket, and he had these sparkly gold shoes with curly toes, and a long white beard."

"Wow!" Chloe laughed, and Lucy could feel herself blushing.

"I'm not making it up," she insisted. "That is what I saw."

"I'm not doubting you, Lucy. I just wish I could have seen him too. You know, in Iceland over half the population believe in elves and dwarfs."

"They do?" Lucy said, breathing hard. "You're not making that up?"

"I'm not. They have actually rerouted roads to avoid disturbing rocks where dwarfs are supposed to live."

"So it's possible?" Lucy said. "That my gnome was real?"

"It's definitely possible," Chloe agreed, which was all Lucy needed to hear.

For the next few minutes, while Chloe went back to

reading, Lucy sat with the bird's nest in her lap. The sun warmed her head, and there was a lovely smell of apples from the windfalls on the grass behind her. When Chloe shifted her legs, Lucy noticed a little gray elephant tattooed on the outside of her shin, right above her left ankle. Once Lucy had discovered it, she couldn't drag her eyes away.

"So is that your best friend who doesn't believe in magic anymore?" Chloe suddenly asked. "The girl you're always with?"

"Yes, that's Ella." Lucy sighed. "She's become a sparkle girl, and now she has new friends she'd rather be with."

"Ahhhhh." Chloe nodded, picking at her nail polish.

"It was awful at school today," Lucy admitted, surprised by how easy it was to tell Chloe stuff. "I didn't know who to talk to at recess."

"Take a book with you tomorrow. That's what I used to do. Then you can read or pretend to read. It makes recess whiz by for lonely kids."

"There's a girl in my class who reads at recess," Lucy said, feeling guilty that she hadn't been friendlier to Rachel. Lucy had never thought of Rachel as lonely before, just as quiet and a little bit unusual, always lugging around her accordion case as if she were about to head off on a trip. "Well thank you for the advice," she added, thinking this was a good time to leave. "And good luck with getting into college."

"See you around," Chloe replied. "And good luck with your gnome. I hope you see him again."

"I hope so too," Lucy said, regretting all the times she'd run into her house whenever Chloe had appeared outside. That was the one good thing about Mrs. Minor's horrible fence. It had helped her make friends with Chloe. She wasn't nearly as intimidating or weird as she looked. In fact she was actually really nice. And she believed in magic!

9

MRS. CASTOR WAS STILL LYING ON THE SOFA
when Lucy came bounding back inside. She managed a
weak "Hi, Lucy," and groaned. "This nausea is just the worst."

"Perhaps I could make you a potion?" Lucy suggested,
feeling inspired to try some spell making again. "A little
brew to help you feel better, Mom." Before Mrs. Castor could
answer, Lucy had dashed upstairs to her bedroom and tugged
Nature's Magic out of her bookcase. When she reappeared
with the big, dusty book, Mrs. Castor eyed it suspiciously.

"Is that the one you found at the Put and Take?"

"It is," Lucy said with great confidence, sniffing the pages.
There was a strong whiff of mold clinging to the paper, but

behind the dampness Lucy was certain she could smell spices and herbs and something distinctly magical. She had always believed this was a real spell book, and after her conversation with Chloe, Lucy felt determined to give it another go.

Last year she and Ella had pounded mint leaves into a potion to try and cure Ella's hiccups. This was one of the remedies listed in the book, but it didn't really work, because Ella was laughing so hard she kept hiccupping even faster. Although now Lucy realized what the problem might have been. They probably should have said a little spell to go along with the potion.

"Lucy, what exactly are you planning?" Mrs. Castor said rather anxiously, watching Lucy flip through the pages.

"Mom, please don't worry. I know what I'm doing. How about this?" Lucy suggested. "A remedy for upset stomachs?"

"What's in it exactly?"

"Ginger and honey, and a dash of cinnamon." Lucy gave a small sigh. "I just wish they used proper ingredients like eye of newt and spider's breath. Things like that."

"Well, I certainly wouldn't be drinking it if they did."

"I'm going to write you out a spell," Lucy said. "To make the magic work. And you have to say it when you drink the potion, Mom."

"That's fine, Lucy, but no added surprises, please. I don't want to find a fly wing or a spider leg floating in my drink."

Since Mrs. Castor didn't have any fresh ginger lying

around, Lucy decided to use powdered ginger instead. She followed the directions for the recipe, pouring boiling water over the ginger and stirring in some honey and cinnamon. It smelled quite nice, more Christmassy than magical, so while it cooled a bit, Lucy sat down to write a spell. She used a purple pen, because (Lucy felt quite sure) purple was a magical color, and surprisingly the words sort of popped into her head, as if she had no control over them. As if they had definitely arrived there by magic.

"Here you go," Lucy said, handing her mother a mug and a piece of paper. "It's quite safe," she added as Mrs. Castor peered into her drink.

"Just ginger, honey, and cinnamon. Right, Lucy?"

"Yes." Lucy nodded at the bit of paper. "And that's the spell, Mom, which is very important, so please try to use a proper chanting voice when you say it."

Under Lucy's eager gaze Mrs. Castor took a tiny, cautious sip, and then holding up the paper she said, "Bubble, boil, a magic brew, to make me feel as good as new. Soon I will be up to bake, Lucy's favorite chocolate cake."

"Very good." Lucy beamed at her mother, who had started to laugh. "How do you feel? You definitely sound much more cheerful."

"It is rather soothing," Mrs. Castor agreed, taking another sip. "Thank you, Lucy."

Even though Mrs. Castor said she felt better, there was

still no sign of chocolate cake baking by the time Mr. Castor came home from the high school.

"Hey, it's Monday," Lucy said as her father put a pizza box down on the kitchen table, along with a stack of papers he needed to mark. Pizza night was always on Friday nights, half cheese, half pepperoni, and Lucy looked at her mother in alarm. "Mom, where's the spaghetti?" Lucy asked. "We always have spaghetti on Mondays."

"Can you make an exception, Lucy?" Mr. Castor said, rumpling up his hair. His eyes looked red and his shirt had come untucked. "Your mom isn't up to cooking right now."

"Well, she should be," Lucy said. "I just made her a very powerful magic potion."

"And it has helped my nausea," Mrs. Castor insisted. "But I'm not quite ready to face spaghetti yet, Lucy. Plus, I'm so behind on my kangaroo features page."

"Which is why we need to find someone to come in and help out a bit," Lucy's dad said, glancing at Lucy's mom. "With the cooking and cleaning, I mean, so you can get your work done. At least until you feel better."

"Hope they can make spaghetti," Lucy whispered.

"I thought you'd be pleased," Mr. Castor said. "Pizza is a treat."

"A Friday treat," Lucy pointed out softly, but she didn't complain anymore, because her father looked as if he had had a difficult first day of school too.

It was a quiet meal. Lucy's mother didn't join them, and Lucy's dad seemed to be thinking about other things. There were clock bits all over the table, and the pizza tasted wrong—too much sauce and not enough cheese. Which was no surprise considering it was Monday. Every once in a while Mrs. Castor would lean over Mildred, but when Lucy offered to make her up another potion, she just shook her head and groaned.

Pizza on Monday was bad enough, but when her mother went to bed at the same time as Lucy, it completely upset the nighttime routine. And to make matters worse, her dad seemed to have forgotten to come up and say good night, something that had never happened before. While Lucy waited for him to appear, she checked in her closet to see if her gnome had returned, and then with a heavy sigh Lucy knelt on the floor by her nests.

She picked up the robin's nest and traced a finger along one of the green sparkly threads, feeling something crackle behind it. A piece of newspaper was tucked underneath, hidden among the twigs and leaves and bits of grass. Very gently Lucy wiggled the newspaper out and unfolded the creases. She peered at the tiny writing. *David Ortiz's grand slam at the bottom of the ninth inning was all the magic needed for the Red Sox to win. . . .* Lucy stared at the scrap of newspaper. Goose bumps broke out on her arms and a shiver tickled its way down her spine.

She wasn't sure whom the Red Sox had won against, because the rest of the sentence was missing. But it didn't matter. It didn't matter one bit. All that mattered was that one little word, "magic," hidden inside her nest. A pinch of magic just waiting to be discovered. And Lucy knew this had to be a sign. She couldn't wait to tell Chloe. What was it Chloe had said? Magic was everywhere; you just had to know where to look.

Being very careful not to rip it, Lucy dropped the scrap of newspaper next to the pile of sparkles in the drawer of her bedside table. Then she got out her notebook and on the page opposite her gnome picture, wrote *Magical Signs*. Underneath, Lucy started a list.

1. Seeing a gnome in my cupboard.
2. Finding sparkles from the gnome's shoes on my cupboard floor.
3. Feeling magic in the garden.
4. Making a magic potion that actually *worked*, because my mom definitely felt less sick.
5. Discovering the word "magic" hidden in my robin's nest.

Lucy contemplated putting down the thing Chloe had told her about her mom bumping into her new boyfriend outside Valley Donuts, but it felt a bit like cheating, since it wasn't Lucy's sign. That bit of magic belonged to Chloe's mom.

By the time Lucy had finished her list, Mr. Castor still hadn't come to her room, and it was half an hour past her bedtime. She slipped her notebook back in the drawer and touched the scrap of newspaper. "Magic," Lucy whispered with a shiver. "Ella's wrong. It does exist."

10

THE NEXT DAY AT RECESS LUCY WATCHED ELLA go off with Summer, May, and Molly. It was hard to tell who was who from behind, except that Ella's ponytail was a little blonder than the others. Ella hadn't asked Lucy if she wanted to come with them, although she had been perfectly nice to her in math and smiled when Lucy got the right answer to an extremely difficult problem Ms. Fisher had written on the board.

After wandering around the playground for a bit, Lucy took her book over to the large maple tree and sat down next to Rachel. She opened *The Hobbit* and stared at the page. Somehow, when her parents read the story out loud it made perfect sense, or perfect sense until her dad started falling asleep. But there were too many complicated words, and after struggling through the first paragraph Lucy gave up. Chloe had been right though. Holding a book in your hands was like a shield. It protected you, gave you something to hide behind, and Lucy could watch the sparkle girls practice their hip-hop moves without anyone noticing.

Sitting next to Rachel was actually rather comforting. In fact Lucy wasn't sure Rachel had even noticed she was there. Not until she started laughing. "Must be a funny book," Lucy said.

Rachel looked up, surprised to find Lucy sitting beside her. She hesitated a moment before saying, "It's my favorite book in the world. I've read it twice already."

"Wow, that's impressive."

Glancing around, Rachel asked, "Why aren't you with Ella? You two are always together."

"She's over there. She's become a sparkle girl." Lucy sighed. "I still can't believe it." She picked at a mosquito bite on her leg.

"That is upsetting," Rachel agreed, and Lucy nodded. She didn't want to talk about Ella.

"What's it about, your book?"

Rachel held it out so Lucy could see the title. "I found it at a yard sale when we lived in Georgia," she said. "I couldn't read it then. I just liked the cover. And it's exciting more than funny," Rachel added. "But I always laugh when I'm excited."

"*The Lord of the Rings*!" Lucy exclaimed, wondering if this were another sign. "My neighbor loves that book too. It has an elf princess in it, right?"

"Arwen!" Rachel clutched the book to her chest. "Have you read this?"

"No." Lucy shook her head. "I'm not a good enough reader."

"If you can manage that?" Rachel glanced at *The Hobbit*.

"I can't. My parents are reading it to me," Lucy admitted.

"I love to read. My mom says that's why I need glasses, because I strain my eyes reading under the covers at night. I'm not allowed to but I do it anyway!"

"When did you live in Georgia?" Lucy asked, realizing she knew almost nothing about Rachel. "That's a long way from Hawthorne."

"For a year before moving up here. Before that I lived in Texas and before that San Diego."

"I've only ever lived on Beech Street."

"You're lucky." Rachel made a face. "I hate moving around so much. I was born in Chicago, but I don't remember that because I was only a baby."

Lucy couldn't imagine living in so many different homes. "You must have been to a lot of schools."

"I have." Rachel nodded. "And it's hard to make friends when you're always about to leave somewhere. I suppose that's why I love books so much. Because I can take them with me."

"So how long are you going to be in Hawthorne for?" Lucy asked, thinking that she would be utterly miserable if she had to pack up her nests and move every few years.

Rachel shrugged. "My dad says we're definitely here to stay this time. We moved around so much because of his job, you see, but he has a different job now, so I'm really truly hoping this is it." She glanced at her watch and scrambled to her feet.

"Hey, where are you going?" Lucy said rather anxiously. "Recess isn't over."

"Almost is. I have an accordion lesson during music class, and Ms. Larkin gets all grumpy if I'm late."

"Why do you play?" Lucy asked her, realizing this sounded a little rude.

"You mean because I'm absolutely rubbish at it?"

"I didn't say that." Lucy looked flustered, hoping she hadn't hurt Rachel's feelings. "In fact, you're the best accordion player I know."

"I'm the only accordion player you know." Rachel laughed.

"That is true."

"It belonged to my great-grandpa," Rachel explained.

"He brought it over with him from Hungary when he emi-grated. Everyone says he was an amazing musician, so I'm trying to carry on the family tradition. Which," Rachel added softly, "I have plenty of time to do. Although it is crazy difficult," she confessed. "But I kind of love it too." Smiling and holding *The Lord of the Rings*, she pretended to play an air accordion. "I like to imagine him belting out all these rousing folk tunes."

Lucy was extremely glad Rachel had so much enthusi-asm because (unless she had improved over the summer) her great-grandfather certainly hadn't passed along any of his musical abilities.

"Hey," Rachel suddenly said, stopping to wave her book in front of Lucy. "Can I read this to you next recess? If you like *The Hobbit*, you'll love *The Lord of the Rings*." Lucy stared at her and Rachel's face flushed pink. "Okay, that's weird, isn't it?"

It was a bit weird, Lucy thought, but at least it would give her something to do during recess. "No, I think it's a nice idea," she said.

"You do? Oh good!" Rachel laughed again and Lucy joined in, not understanding what was so funny, but find-ing the laugh infectious.

Lucy had decided not to share her big sister announcement with anyone. Not talking about it meant she didn't have to think about it, and Lucy managed to keep the news to herself . . . until the following Friday morning, when Ella came running up to her as soon as she got to school.

"Why didn't you tell me?" Ella shrieked. "Your mom told my mom, and I can't believe you haven't said anything yet." She flung her arms around Lucy and shrieked some more, as Molly, Summer, and May came hurrying over to join them.

"What's happening?" Summer said.

"Lucy's mom is going to have a baby!" Ella shouted.

"Yay!" Summer squealed, grabbing Lucy by the arms and jumping up and down.

Lucy wondered if she were a terrible person, because she didn't feel so much as a grain of excitement. Nothing like Summer and Ella were showing, and it wasn't even their baby. The other girls started to squeal too, joining in the jumping and making Lucy's head ache.

"What's going on?" Jarmal asked, racing over with his best friend Thomas Blackburn.

"Lucy's mom is going to have a baby," Ella shrieked.

Thomas shook his head. "Sorry about that," he said, noticing Lucy's glum expression. "Not easy being replaced, is it? And wait till it's born," he warned. "It gets worse. Then your parents won't have any time for you. At all. All they do is take pictures of the baby. My dad took two photos with me in them last year and about two thousand of smelly Shelly."

"Don't listen to him," Summer insisted, putting her hands on her hips and giving her ponytail a flip. "He's just trying to scare you, Lucy. Being a big sister is wonderful. That's what I wished for every year on my birthday."

"I'm not trying to scare you, Lucy," Thomas said. "I'm just being honest."

"Thanks, Thomas," Lucy replied in a small voice, wondering why anyone would wish for a baby sister when there were so many other things to ask for, like a Labrador puppy or having proper magical powers.

Coming home from school that afternoon Lucy was walking with her head down, searching for unusual-looking coins that might grant wishes hidden in the cracks of the sidewalk, when she bumped straight into the velvet cloaked figure of Chloe.

"Ouch!" Lucy looked up, stumbling backward. Chloe was all bones and hard angles. She smelled faintly of mothballs and had dyed her hair crimson. Standing beside her was the boy with the hedgehog hair. He wore a leather jacket covered in chains, and a safety pin dangled from his ear. Lucy's heart quickened, and she looked away, not wanting to make eye contact with him.

"Careful." Chloe shot out a hand to steady Lucy. "Look where you're going, yes?"

"Sorry," Lucy apologized, feeling her old discomfort

return, the way it used to whenever she saw Chloe. But then Chloe smiled, and Lucy remembered how nice she was.

"See you then, Chloe, I'm off," the boy said, giving Lucy a friendly grin. He had warm, kind eyes, the color of chestnuts, which Lucy hadn't noticed before, and he suddenly didn't look so scary. "Don't want to be late for work."

"Bye, Jack," Chloe said as she gave him a small wave.

"Stop by for a burger later if you want."

"I might," Chloe replied, and Lucy wondered if Jack were her boyfriend. "He works at the diner," Chloe explained as Jack darted across the street. "We went to school together. We're just friends," Chloe added, as if she could tell what Lucy was thinking. "Anyway, what's up? How are things?"

Lucy shrugged. "Okay, I guess." She glanced away for a moment. "But I've been dying to tell you, Chloe. I'm collecting signs of magic!" Lucy described the scrap of newspaper she had found in her nest, and Chloe looked suitably impressed.

"And your book idea was really great," Lucy continued. "That girl Rachel I told you about, the one who reads at recess, is actually kind of nice. She's very different from Ella." Lucy paused a moment. "I really miss Ella. Well, I miss the old Ella. But guess what? Rachel is reading me *Lord of the Rings.* It's her favorite book in the whole world, just like you. Do you think that might be a sign?"

"I think that's someone you should pay attention to,"

Chloe said. "I'm certainly impressed. I didn't read *Lord of the Rings* until two years ago. I was sixteen!"

"Well, Rachel's really smart. I'm not sure if she believes in magic though. I haven't asked her, but I wouldn't be surprised if she does. She certainly likes reading about it."

"So what else is going on?" Chloe said bluntly. "Because I can tell you've got something on your mind."

"Those O'Brien boys are so annoying." Lucy sighed. "I can hear them from my bedroom. And the Toad is always crying."

Chloe grinned. "They are loud, but at least they're not on our side of the street. You can't let that upset you, Lucy."

Lucy stared at her shoes, feeling the tips of her ears start to throb. "My mom is going to have a baby," she said. Then before she could stop herself, Lucy added, "I'd much rather we were getting a dog." Thankfully, Chloe didn't say anything remotely perky. In fact she didn't say anything at all. She just gave Lucy a sympathetic look, which showed that she understood. "So did you hear about college yet?" Lucy asked, wanting to change the subject.

"I've got an interview!" Chloe gave a little jump, which was most un-Chloe-like. "And I'm so excited because some people don't even get that far. They get rejected right away. It's not for a few weeks though, which is good, because I'm making something really amazing to wear and I'm nowhere near finished." She held out her arms so the cloak fabric draped down like bat wings. "I thought I'd take this along to show them too. It's a sort of elf princess cloak. I love the chocolaty brown color. You could blend into the forest wearing it, couldn't you? I found the fabric at the Put and Take. That place is magic!" Chloe said. "I always come across exactly what I need."

"Oh, I know. My dad and I love the Put and Take," Lucy cried. "I've found some of my best treasures there. And it is magic, Chloe. You're right."

"This used to be an old pair of curtains," Chloe said, swirling around in her bat cloak. "They must have been stored in someone's attic for a while though, because they stunk of mothballs."

"I'd wear that all the time if I had one," Lucy said. "You're going to be famous, Chloe."

"I have to find a job first." Chloe sighed. "To help pay for college. That is, if I get in, of course. And if I don't get in, I'm going to need a job anyway." She paused and sighed again. "It's tough out there right now. I've applied to all the stores in town but no one is hiring. Jack even tried to get me a job at the diner, but they don't need anyone."

"You could come and work for us," Lucy offered, knowing as soon as the words were out of her mouth that she should probably have asked her parents first. Still, Chloe needed a job and her mom needed help, so it seemed like a sensible idea. "The baby is making my mom feel really sick, and she's looking for someone to help with the chores."

"I'd love to," Chloe said, running her purple nails through her tomato-colored hair. "Gosh, that would be so fantastic."

"Can you make spaghetti?"

"I guess." Chloe shrugged.

"Perhaps Jack could teach you, since he's a cook. Why don't you come around later?" Lucy told her. "I'm sure my parents will be thrilled."

"You asked who?" Mrs. Castor said when Lucy told her what she'd done. She was sprawled in an armchair, Mildred wedged at her feet. Even with all the lights on, the kitchen was dark and gloomy as the inside of a shoe box.

"I thought you'd be pleased," Lucy said. "You were the one who told me Chloe was nice under all her makeup. And you were right, Mom. She is really nice and she's trying to save money for college. She hasn't got in yet, but I'm sure she will. Chloe is so clever. She makes all her own clothes." There was a rather long silence. "I know what you're thinking," Lucy continued when her mother didn't speak. "You're remembering the time she came home in a police car, aren't you?"

"And the fact that she's covered in piercings and never smiles," Mrs. Castor murmured.

"That's what I used to think," Lucy said. "But then I

realized I never smiled at her, so why should she be the one to smile first? And you always told me you shouldn't judge people by their appearances."

"Let's see what your father says, shall we?" Mrs. Castor replied, not looking at all sure about Lucy's idea.

Mr. Castor didn't seem very sure either. "I taught Chloe history," he said, giving Lucy's mom one of those private grown-up looks. "She's been through a hard time with her parents divorcing and everything. But I don't know . . ."

"Well, I like her," Lucy said. "And she can make spaghetti."

"Then I think we should give her a chance," Mrs. Castor said, suddenly making up her mind. "Because the way I'm feeling, I'm not going to be cooking spaghetti again for a very long while."

11

LUCY WAS GLAD CHLOE WORE HER LEAF DRESS
when she came over that evening, because it was bound
to make a good impression on Lucy's parents and show
them how talented Chloe was. To begin with Chloe had on
her serious face and didn't say much, but Lucy could tell
this was because she was nervous, since she kept crumpling
one of the leaves on her dress into a tight ball, ruining its
smooth flutteriness.

Lucy kept grinning at her, hoping Chloe would mirror
her expression and smile back, and when she finally did,
Chloe's whole face lit up and she looked all friendly and nice
and not the least bit intimidating. Lucy laughed in relief,

sure that everything would be okay now, and she munched on a ginger cookie while Chloe talked about how much she wanted to go to college and design her own clothes. She even stood up and swirled (which was Lucy's suggestion), so the Castors could see how beautiful her dress was.

As soon as Chloe heard she had got the job, she hugged all the Castors with great passion, and after she left, Mr. Castor said it was like being hugged by a tree. "But you were right, Lucy," he added quickly, to show that he was joking. "Chloe is nice. She was such a quiet child when they moved here, I don't remember much about her. And she's much chattier than the Chloe I had in my history class."

Chloe came every day for a couple of hours, and although she wasn't the best cleaner in the world, she had plenty of enthusiasm, tidying all Mr. Castor's carefully arranged clock bits off the kitchen table and polishing one of the side tables so hard that a leg broke right off. Her cooking wasn't the best either, and Lucy secretly began to think that pizza on Mondays might actually be better than spaghetti made by Chloe.

"Hey, where did this come from?" Chloe said one afternoon, picking *Nature's Magic* up from the coffee table. It had been buried for the past few days under a pile of kangaroo library books.

"I found it at the Put and Take," Lucy said, looking up from her math homework. She was wondering whether to tell Chloe that it might very possibly be a real spell book, when Chloe said, "This is so cool, Lucy. All these old herbal remedies. It probably belonged to a witch!"

"Chloe, that's just what I think," Lucy cried.

"I mean, seriously," Chloe went on. "I bet these were the sort of things the Salem witches used to brew." Lucy knew all about the Salem witches from her father. They were a group of women who lived a long time ago in Salem, Massachusetts, accused of practicing magic.

"Lucy made me some ginger tea from in there," Mrs. Castor remarked, looking over from the Nest. "It really helped with my nausea."

"But you need to say a spell to go along with them," Lucy said. "Ella and I tried a hiccup potion without the magic, and it didn't work."

"Interesting," Chloe murmured, slowly turning the pages. "Where do you get the spells from?"

"I don't know." Lucy shrugged. "They just pop into my head." And then lowering her voice she whispered, "I think I might actually have magic powers, Chloe."

"Wouldn't surprise me one bit," Chloe said, smiling at Lucy.

It was wonderful that Chloe also believed in magic, but the best thing about her was that she didn't keep mentioning the baby or trying to convince Lucy how great it was going to be. Nor did Rachel, thank goodness. At recess the girls would sit under the maple tree, which was starting to turn a deep crimson, while Rachel read *The Lord of the Rings* out loud, and if it rained they perched on one of the class windowsills. Although Lucy still didn't know Rachel that well, she found her extremely easy to be with. One rainy Tuesday they had just reached the part in the book where Arwen, princess of the elves, decides to marry Aragorn and give up her immortality, when Lucy turned to Rachel and whispered, "Do you believe in elves and magic?" She spoke softly so the sparkle girls wouldn't hear.

"I don't know." Rachel tilted her head. "Maybe. I like the idea of magic."

"Chloe, my next-door neighbor, says that half the population in Iceland believe in elves and dwarfs," Lucy whispered. "For real, I mean."

"Really?" Rachel looked intrigued. "Well, then I guess it's possible."

"Look at this," Lucy said, feeling brave enough to get out her notebook. She showed Rachel her gnome drawing. "That's what I saw in my closet. And I found some sparkles from his shoes on the floor."

"Ahh, he's so sweet, Lucy," Rachel said, and Lucy wasn't sure if that meant Rachel believed her or not.

"I did see him," she said firmly. "But I don't want anyone else to know."

"I won't say a word," Rachel whispered, handing her back the notebook. "Your gnome is safe with me. And when I get home, I'm going to look up Icelandic dwarfs on my dad's computer. That is so interesting."

Some days Ella would come charging over to Lucy and Rachel, full of sparkle energy, and want an update on Lucy's baby news. Had they thought of names yet? Was it a boy or a girl? If it was a girl, what about calling her Peaches because that was a beautiful name? It was always a relief when Ella rushed off again, back to Summer and Molly and May, because Lucy could relax and be herself.

One afternoon, walking home from school, Lucy had turned onto Beech Street and was wandering along thinking about how many other houses might have resident gnomes living in them, when Mrs. O'Brien came driving past in her great big minivan. A few moments later the lovely peace was broken as she parked in her usual place, right opposite the Castors', and boys started exploding out of the back like popcorn.

"Micky, Billy, do not go near the road," Mrs. O'Brien hollered, hauling a wiggling Toady out of his car seat. "Sammy, watch them, please." Sammy appeared to be paying no attention, zooming around the yard in a Batman cape with his arms spread out like wings. He was making "pow, pow" noises and doing karate kicks, while Micky and Billy chased after him, making even louder "pow, pow" noises. Lucy watched in horror as Billy stopped for a moment to wipe his little cardboard book across his nose.

"Hi, Lucy. Want to take that lot home with you?" Mrs. O'Brien called out. Lucy's mouth dropped open and Mrs. O'Brien laughed. "I'm only joking, Lucy. But honestly, I can't wait until you're old enough to babysit."

Lucy smiled weakly. This was not the first time Mrs. O'Brien had mentioned babysitting, and at some point (even though Lucy hated hurting people's feelings) she would have to tell her that this was never, ever, under any circumstances, going to happen. Toady was staring at Lucy, and she tried making a happy face, which triggered a loud howl.

"He's got a bit of a tummy ache," Mrs. O'Brien said kindly. Although Lucy knew it had nothing to do with tummy aches. Toady didn't like her any more than she liked him.

"I have to go, Mrs. O'Brien," Lucy said. Micky started crying because Sammy had accidentally karate kicked him in the face, and escaping while she had the chance, Lucy dashed across the street to her house.

She found her mother slumped in the big armchair, studying a book of baby names.

"If our baby is like Toady, we're sending it back," Lucy announced, dropping her bag on the floor. "I cannot live with one of those." Mrs. Castor glanced up from the name book and smiled. "So no cake for tea?" Lucy continued. "Not that I mind or anything. I completely understand with you being so ill and everything. It's just that Chloe isn't a cake maker, and I do miss them." Chloe, the Castors had come to find out, was barely a kettle boiler, let alone a cake maker. But she was trying, Lucy noticed, eyeing the plate of burnt cookies on the table.

"This won't go on forever, Lucy, I promise," Mrs. Castor said.

Lucy picked up a cookie and tried to bite into it. It was a bit like eating a rock. Jack clearly wasn't being much help in the cooking lesson department. "Have you chosen a name yet?" she asked her mother, glancing at the book.

"No, but it's exciting to think about them. It helps me remember that this is all going to be worth it." Lucy forced herself to smile, which was hard to do when she didn't feel like smiling and had a hard, burnt cookie in her mouth. "I have to say I rather like traditional names," Mrs. Castor went on. "Elizabeth for a girl, maybe, and William for a boy?"

"Really?" Lucy said, trying to squelch the flame of jealousy flickering in her belly. William and Elizabeth were royal names. Names you gave to kings and queens. Not like common old, garden-variety Lucy. Who ever heard of Queen Lucy Mouse? "I sort of like Rover or Fido myself," Lucy proposed rather hopefully. "Those are comforting, friendly names, don't you think?" She could cope with a Rover or a Fido in the house but not a William or Elizabeth demanding all the attention.

"I'm having a baby, not a dog," Mrs. Castor said.

Lucy gave up on the cookie and took out her homework, wishing it were a cute yellow Labrador curled up inside her mother's tummy.

When Mr. Castor got home he suggested supper in the garden, since the weather was September warm and the kitchen table had a new clock project all over it.

"That's a wonderful idea," Lucy said, giving her father a hug. "Picnics always make things better, especially if it's fried chicken and cherry pie."

"I'm afraid that's a bit of a stretch, Lucy," Mr. Castor admitted. "I was thinking more of sandwiches."

"Well, sandwiches are good too," Lucy said, trying to make the best of things. But once they were outside, she couldn't help worrying, because the petunias on the shady side of the yard looked all wilty and sad, and the roses were shedding petals on the ground. "The flowers hate that fence," Lucy said rather fiercely, sitting on the tartan picnic rug in between her parents. "They are dying from sadness."

"It's also the end of summer, Lucy," Mrs. Castor said.

"No." Lucy shook her head. "They are not getting enough sun."

"Have a tuna fish sandwich," Mr. Castor offered, handing her the plate.

"I am not complaining," Lucy said, taking the smallest sandwich. "And please don't take this the wrong way, because I'm very grateful you made me dinner, and I'll still help with the washing up afterward, but I do think you should know that tuna fish is my second to least favorite thing to eat. It smells all fishy and tastes a bit like cat food."

"Have you ever eaten cat food, Lucy?" Mr. Castor inquired.

"No, I haven't, but if I did, then I think this is just what it would taste like."

"Well, thank you for sharing," Mrs. Castor murmured, putting down her sandwich and sipping at her water.

"A ham sandwich would have been delightful," Lucy whispered. "Or even plain bread and butter."

The rest of the picnic was rather silent. Her father didn't tell any jokes, and Mrs. Castor had brought the book of baby names out with her. She kept glancing at the pages and giving little private smiles. Every once in a while she would say "What about Edward?" or "I quite like Louise," until Lucy felt like picking up the book and flinging it as hard as she could over Mrs. Minor's horrible fence.

12

MUCH TO LUCY'S DELIGHT, MRS. CASTOR HAD purchased a large bag of fresh ginger so she could make up regular batches of ginger tea (or "magic potion," as Lucy liked to call it) for herself. The problem was she kept forgetting to say Lucy's spell when she drank it, which was probably why there was still a distinct lack of chocolate cake in the Castor household. Lucy tried her hardest to make the best of things, but it wasn't easy. Her mother was tired all the time, and behind in her work, and this made her snap at Lucy for stuff she would never have snapped at before.

"I asked you to put your laundry away, Lucy, and to pick up your pens from the floor," Mrs. Castor had grumbled one afternoon, peering out from behind her laptop.

This was quite unfair, Lucy thought, because her mother had never minded about Lucy's grand art projects that lay sprawled across the floor for days. And Chloe had done the laundry only that morning, so it wasn't as if it had been hanging around for weeks like her mother made it seem.

And Mr. Castor, who never worried about things, seemed to be worrying rather a lot these days—about how Lucy's mother was feeling and what a big change this was going to be for them all. Much to Lucy's horror he suddenly started to sound a lot like Grandpa Castor had sounded when he was alive, all stressy and tense. Worst of all, he hadn't read *The Hobbit* three nights in a row, saying he was just too tired. And he wasn't even the one with a baby in his stomach.

One Thursday after school, about seven weeks since Chloe had begun working for the Castors, Lucy was closeted away in her bedroom, suffering from hunger and crankiness in equal amounts. Her dad wasn't home yet, and her mom had completely taken over the Nest, sprawled across it with her laptop. She had snapped rather sharply when Lucy asked if there were any "edible" things to eat in the house, which Lucy still thought was a fair question, since Chloe's burnt cookies, a box of stale cereal, and a couple of too soft pears did not really qualify as "edible," in her opinion.

And then her mother had snapped even more sharply

when Lucy asked her to play Monopoly, saying she had far too much work to finish up. To make matters worse Lucy hadn't seen any signs of magic lately, which was becoming a bit of a worry. Rachel had tried to help by pointing out that she was finally learning a polka tune on the accordion, and not just scales, and that was pretty magical, wasn't it? It was, Lucy agreed. Although secretly she felt this was more miracle than magical, but she was still very happy for her friend.

Going upstairs, Lucy decided to blow the dust off her nest collection and rearrange them. Her favorite nest was also the smallest, a tiny hummingbird nest, no bigger than a walnut, which Lucy had discovered in their backyard last spring. Mrs. Castor had left a shirt of her husband's hanging on the line to dry, and then, as she often did with the washing, forgot to bring it back in. Mr. Castor's shirt had hung outside for a whole week when Lucy noticed that hummingbirds had built a little nest in the top pocket.

Hummingbirds often built their nests in unusual places, a fact Lucy had read all about in *Amazing Animals* magazine. So the shirt stayed right there on the line with the little mama hummingbird sitting on her eggs, until one day, when Lucy came down for breakfast and saw that the family had finally gone. It occurred to her as she knelt beside the shelf, that this had been a pretty magical moment, finding the miniature nest in her dad's shirt. Especially since she'd been wishing really hard for a nest to add to her collection. And even though it had happened last spring, Lucy opened up her notebook (which she had started to carry around with her, just in case) and wrote, *Wish granted— Hummingbird nest appears in shirt pocket*, because you couldn't ignore a wish that had come true.

She was right in the middle of admiring her second favorite nest, the oriole nest her grandmother had brought her back from Maryland two years ago, when Lucy heard the front door open and voices downstairs in the hall.

"Lucy?" her dad called up.

"I'm rather busy right now," Lucy called out, putting the deep pouch-shaped nest back on the shelf. Her grandmother had told her that orioles built their nests to dangle down from the branches, securing them in place with little woven loops. Lucy always thought how fun it must be to swing in an oriole's nest, like a cradle being rocked by the wind.

"Chloe's here," Mr. Castor added. "With some rather good-looking brownies she made!"

"Oh, coming!" Lucy shouted, scrambling to her feet. "Coming right now." She had completely forgotten that Chloe had promised to stop by that afternoon and show them the outfit she was planning to wear for her interview tomorrow.

Charging down the stairs, Lucy bounded into the

kitchen, where Chloe stood by the table in a gauzy blue dress, holding a plate of brownies. She had dyed her hair blue to match her outfit. The top half of the dress was a pale sky color that darkened to a deep ocean-blue in the skirt. Putting the brownies down on the table, Chloe twirled around, looking as if she were rising out of the mist. "Wait till you see the hat I made to go with this," she told them.

Lucy oohed in delight. "You look beautiful, Chloe, like an elf princess of the lake. And the brownies look exactly like brownies should look. Well done!" She plopped down on a chair at the exact moment Chloe cried out.

"NO! My hat. You're on my hat," Chloe wailed as Lucy felt something squish underneath her. Leaping to her feet, she stared at the white plastic bag on the chair.

"I, I didn't know . . . ," Lucy began, watching Chloe pull a crushed gray-looking thing out of the bag.

"Oh, Lucy!" Mr. and Mrs. Castor said together.

"It's ruined," Chloe choked out. "My papier-mâché hat. And it looked just like a river stone, perched on my head."

"We can glue it," Lucy said, her throat filling with lumps. "My dad's a great gluer."

"We can certainly try," Mr. Castor agreed, but Chloe shook her head, stuffing the pieces back in the bag.

"I'll help you make another one," Lucy whispered.

"There's no time, Lucy. My interview's tomorrow morning." Lucy could hear the crossness in Chloe's voice, and bursting into tears, Lucy crawled under the table.

"Oh, this is a nightmare," Lucy sobbed. "You must be so mad at me, Chloe. And I don't blame you. I don't blame you one bit. I am a thoughtless, clumsy person, and I have ruined your beautiful hat.

"I was just so excited to try your brownies," Lucy added, her voice full of quivers. She buried her head in her lap and wrapped her arms around her knees, listening to the soft murmur of her parents telling Chloe how sorry they were. "So I guess this means our friendship is over?" Lucy whispered. "You will never be speaking to me again?"

"Lucy, it's okay," Chloe said with a sigh, bending down and offering her the plate of brownies. "I shouldn't have put my hat on the chair. It wasn't a smart place. And I don't have to wear one to the interview," she added. "I just thought it would look nice."

"Now they'll be able to see how pretty your hair looks," Lucy said, sniffing. She took a brownie, because Chloe had gone to all the trouble of making them and bringing them over, although she didn't feel in a brownie eating mood anymore. "I'd like to hug you," Lucy said, "but I don't want to get chocolate on your dress."

"No, I don't want that either," Chloe replied, darting away from Lucy. "I should go," she murmured, twisting her fingers together. "I have to be up early tomorrow." She gave a soft sigh, and Lucy hated how sad Chloe looked, even though she was trying so hard to hide it.

"Wait a second," Lucy said. "I'll be right back." She had to do something for Chloe, something that would make up for crushing her interview hat. If Chloe didn't get offered a place at college, it might all be Lucy's fault—because her outfit wasn't fancy enough now, or what if Chloe came across as all grumpy and uninterested because she was still feeling sad? Lucy ran upstairs to her room and picked up the robin's nest from her shelf, the one she had taken from Mrs. Minor's tree. She stared at it for a long moment before carrying it carefully back down to the kitchen.

"This is for you," Lucy said, offering the nest to Chloe. "It really should be yours anyway, since it has your ribbons in it. And bits of your hair," she added, feeling a great pang of sadness at saying good-bye to her robin's nest. But that was good, Lucy decided. It balanced out the sadness that Chloe must be feeling right now.

"Oh, Lucy, I can't take your nest," Chloe said, finally cracking a smile. "I know how special this is to you. It's your magic nest."

"I want you to have it," Lucy insisted, putting the nest into Chloe's hands. "You need the magic more than I do. It will bring you luck." She had a worrying feeling Chloe might not want to work for the Castors anymore, and that would be just terrible, since hers was the only cheerful face Lucy saw around the house these days.

After Chloe had gone, Mr. and Mrs. Castor sat with Lucy on the couch, trying to make her feel better. "You didn't mean to, Lucy," Mrs. Castor murmured softly. "We all know that."

"Accidents happen," her father agreed. And for a few short minutes it was just like old times, all of them cuddled together on the Nest, even though Mrs. Castor had splayed out starfish style, taking up most of the room. But then Lucy's mother started to feel sick again and had to balance Mildred on her knees, and Lucy's dad began to go through the mail, giving soft stressy sighs every once in a while. No one felt like eating brownies. Which was a pity, Lucy thought, because they were actually quite good, and not the least bit burnt.

As she sat there, squished between her parents, she couldn't help thinking how clever hummingbirds were. So much cleverer than people, because they used spiderwebs when they built their nests, weaving the sticky threads in with thistledown. This meant that as the baby humming-birds grew, their nest could expand to contain them all. Not like the sofa, Lucy thought, which was already starting to feel far too small for the three of them.

13

AS LUCY SAT AT THE TABLE THE NEXT MORN-ing, spooning up cereal and stuffing homework into her backpack, there was a loud knock on the door. Since Lucy's mom was still upstairs and Lucy's dad had left early for a staff meeting, Lucy raced to open it in a panic. No one visited this early, and she hoped nothing awful had happened to her dad. "Please don't be a policeman bringing bad news," Lucy whispered, tugging open the door. "Oh, Chloe. It's you!" Lucy cried in relief. She gave a happy little skip and then froze, putting her hands up to her cheeks. "Oh, Chloe," she said again, staring at their neighbor's head. "It's, it's . . ." Lucy sighed in delight. "It's magnificent!"

"Do you really like it?" Chloe asked, looking pleased. "You don't mind, do you?"

"That is the most magical hat ever. I'm sure they'll give you a place at college as soon as they see it." Perched on Chloe's head was the upside down robin's nest, and woven in among the grasses and plant stems were threads of ribbon and wool in every possible shade of blue, from sea green to turquoise to indigo and navy. Chloe had left in the bits of lime green ribbon, and the effect was truly dazzling.

"I'm hoping the magic works," Chloe said, glancing over her shoulder at a vintage orange Beetle car with a huge rainbow stenciled on the side. It was parked out front, and Jack waved at them through the window. "Hi, Lucy," he called out.

Chloe rolled her eyes. "Jack borrowed that car from his gran. It's ancient but it still runs. Jack and Mel are taking me to Boston for good luck." Mel, the girl with the long dark hair, leaned out of a back window, and Lucy decided that black lipstick was not a cheerful look.

"Come on, Chloe," Mel shouted. "You don't want to be late, and it's going to take us hours in this thing."

"Coming, Mel. Keep your fingers crossed, Lucy," Chloe said.

"And my toes," Lucy called after her as Chloe wafted down the path, her blue dress swirling out from under her velvet cape.

Chloe's hat was without question a perfect petunia moment. And there had been very few of them since her parents' big announcement eight weeks ago. The sad thing was Mr. and Mrs. Castor had not even been there to enjoy it. Lucy sensed this lack of petunia moments was bad for their health, although she didn't know what to do about it.

It had crossed Lucy's mind that her whole family might be suffering from a disorder called SAD. Lucy had read about SAD in one of the Sunday newspapers. It had been the headline story in the lifestyles section. She didn't read the entire article, because it was rather long, but she read enough to get the general idea. Apparently, if you didn't get sufficient sunlight, it could make you depressed. A lot of people got SAD in the winter, Lucy remembered the headlines saying, and you could treat it by sitting under a special sort of sunlamp that made you feel happy again.

Well, ever since Mrs. Minor had put up her fence, there had been a distinct lack of happiness in the Castors' house. Maybe it wasn't just the baby coming that was making everyone grumpy? Maybe it was a serious lack of sunshine, Lucy thought. And maybe if she could find a solution, it would make her parents start smiling again and realize what an amazing daughter they already had. She did con-sider knocking the fence down (or trying to), but Lucy knew this would get her into a great deal of trouble and would probably create more grumpiness, not less.

It turned out to be at the Put and Take, a couple of days later, that Lucy found the answer she was looking for. She had stopped in on her way home from school to see if there were any interesting treasures. Over the years, along with her genie lamp, magic carpet, and spell book, she had acquired a ceramic whale with a chipped blow-hole, a wooden tennis racket, and her book of strange but true facts.

Today though, stamping wet leaves off her shoes, it was the cans of paint sitting on the table that immediately caught her eye. She could tell how bright and lovely the colors were from the drips down the sides, and Lucy read the names out loud. "Shock Your Socks Off Green, Purple Explosion, Electric Pink, Groovy Orange, Zoom to the Moon Blue, and Sunburst Yellow."

It was the Sunburst Yellow that made her smile return. She would paint the kitchen yellow as a surprise. This had to be a sign, Lucy thought, goose bumps breaking out on her arms. Standing very still she could feel that electric, pulsing sensation in the air that happened whenever there was magic around. Only last week Lucy's mother had mentioned how nice it would be to "redo" the kitchen, and here, in answer to her wish, was a beautiful tub of Sunburst Yellow, just waiting for Lucy to take home. "I always knew the Put and Take had to be magic!" Lucy whispered, determined to give her genie lamp another rub later on.

With Sunburst-colored walls it would feel as if the sun were shining even if they couldn't actually see it, and this would be bound, Lucy felt certain, to lift everyone's spirits up again. She gave the can a shake, not surprised to discover it was nicely heavy, and holding the tin in her arms Lucy nudged open the door. A bitter wind blew in her face. She had to be careful not to slip on the damp leaves scattered across the sidewalk.

There were pumpkins everywhere, on front porches and gateposts, and Lucy realized it was almost Halloween. Usually this was one of her favorite holidays, dressing up with Ella in matching costumes. They always carved pumpkins together and frightened themselves silly, daring each other to knock on Mrs. Minor's door for candy. This year though, Lucy knew Ella was going trick-or-treating with the sparkle girls. May was having a party first, which Lucy hadn't been invited to, and as she walked home she was hit by a sudden pang of sadness, missing the old Ella and Lucy, wanting things back the way they used to be.

Why did Ella have to go and change? Lucy thought angrily, kicking at a stone. To stop the mournful feelings from bubbling up, Lucy concentrated on how she could manage to keep her surprise a secret from her parents. What if she painted first thing in the morning perhaps, before her mom and dad were up? She'd set her alarm clock for five—no, six—Lucy decided. Five was awfully early, and it surely couldn't take more than half an hour to paint their little kitchen, could it?

"Big art project?" Chloe said, meeting Lucy at the Castors' front door. She was on her way out, dressed in tight brown leggings and a green velvet tunic. Apart from the blue hair and pierced bits Chloe looked surprisingly elflike.

"Sssh," Lucy whispered, putting a finger to her lips. "It's going to be a surprise for Mom and Dad. To cheer them up."

"What are you painting?" Chloe asked, a hint of nervousness in her voice.

"You'll see tomorrow," Lucy whispered. "But everyone's going to love it! This is a sign, Chloe." Lucy patted the tin. "It was just sitting at the Put and Take waiting for me to find. Things are going to be a lot brighter around here. In fact you're going to need to bring your sunglasses when you come over in the morning."

Lucy smiled and said, "I'm making the best of things. Just like you did with the nest hat." She shifted the can of paint to a more comfortable position, trying not to think about Ella, or May's party, or Halloween at all. "Have you heard from Prachets yet?"

"No, but I'm feeling hopeful." Chloe grinned. "They did all love my outfit."

"And you were wearing your magic hat. You'll get a place," Lucy said. "I'm not worried."

Chloe hesitated on the doorstep a moment longer. She kept glancing at the can of yellow paint. "Are you're sure you wouldn't like my help?"

"I'm good, Chloe. Thanks." Lucy inched past her and dropped her backpack on the hall floor. She gave a little wave. "Just don't forget your sunglasses in the morning," she whispered.

14

L UCY HID THE CAN OF YELLOW PAINT ON THE floor of the hall coat cupboard. She was glad of her cheering up plan because the house seemed gloomier than usual. Some of the clocks had stopped ticking, Lucy noticed, which made it feel as if the heartbeat of the house were slowly fading. Mr. Castor kept forgetting to wind them. Lucy did her best to keep the important clocks going, the station clock and the grandfather clock, but some of the smaller clocks looked absolutely miserable, Lucy thought, their hands stuck at all the wrong times.

When she walked into the kitchen, Lucy found her mother asleep on the Nest, sprawled right across it, so there was no room for Lucy to sit down. Mr. Castor was lying on his back under the sink, fiddling about with a wrench. He had a free period at the end of the day on Wednesdays, so instead of helping out with soccer practice like he usually did in the fall, he came right home.

"Hello," Lucy said, working to keep her voice cheerful.

"There's a leak under this sink," Mr. Castor said, poking his head out. "I'm attempting to fix the stupid thing." Mr. Castor never said "stupid," and Lucy thought about pointing out that he was so busy trying to get things done, he was forgetting to smell the petunias. But one look at his tired face and she decided it was best not to mention this. Tomorrow, when her parents walked into the kitchen, they would both start smiling again. They had to, Lucy reasoned, as soon as they saw the Sunburst Yellow walls.

Lucy set her alarm clock for six, but she was so excited to get painting that she woke at five thirty, her eyes popping open all by themselves. This felt like the greatest idea ever, and Lucy hummed softly as she retrieved the paint from the coat cupboard and tiptoed into the kitchen, trying to be as quiet as she could manage. It would ruin the surprise if her parents discovered what she was up to before she had finished.

Leaving the can on a chair, Lucy opened the back door and padded across the damp grass in her bare feet, heading toward the little garden shed in the corner of the yard. This was where her father kept his work supplies, and she rooted around the shelves, pushing aside rolls of string and jars of screws until she found what she was looking for. There was a whole box of paintbrushes and rollers, all different sizes. Lucy studied them for a minute before helping herself to a large, wide brush and a smaller, narrower one. Then hurrying back to the kitchen she knelt down beside the can of paint and used a spoon end to pry the lid off.

"Ohhhh," Lucy murmured as she peered inside. The paint was brighter than she'd expected. A lot brighter. It had a dazzling glow about it that made Lucy think of summer days when the light was so sharp it hurt your eyes. She stirred the paint about with the spoon. It looked good enough to eat, like melted lemon ice cream. Putting the spoon down on the back of an envelope, Lucy picked up the big brush and dipped it in. Yellow paint dripped on the floor as she walked over to the wall between the two windows and started to paint. It would be more convenient, Lucy realized, to move the can closer, so she put it on the rug by her feet. She had stepped in some of the paint drops and spread them about, but it would be easier to clean up all the mess at the end.

The first few strokes looked lovely, and right away the room felt brighter. This was just like a big art project, Lucy thought, although you could see all her brushstrokes, and when Lucy's dad painted, his walls always looked smooth as butter. Drops of Sunburst Yellow spattered over her nightgown and face as she painted, and she could taste paint on her lips. Lucy wiped her mouth on her sleeve, thinking that this painting business was actually a lot harder than it looked.

The station clock struck seven, and Lucy gave a little start. Her parents would be up soon and she hadn't nearly finished. She hadn't even filled up the space between the windows, and Lucy started to feel rather nervous as she stood back to examine her handiwork. It looked like a bright yellow mess, splattered in the middle of the wall. In fact it looked a bit like a large, exploding sun, and picking up the small brush Lucy made long, shaky spokes coming out from the center. She would turn it into a proper sun, shining in the middle of the wall.

A knot of panic had formed in Lucy's stomach, and she was just wondering whether there might be time to wash it all off, when footsteps came treading down the stairs. As Mr. Castor pushed open the door, he stood in silence for a long moment, staring at Lucy and the wall. Lucy guessed by the expression on her father's face that this had not been a good idea, and she knew it for sure when he shouted her name so loud that her mother appeared soon afterward.

"Whatever have you done?" Mrs. Castor wailed, grabbing the back of a chair. "Good grief, Lucy, what a mess. What an absolute mess."

"I was trying to surprise you," Lucy said. "I wanted to do something special." Her lip had started to tremble. "I thought you'd be happy," she added. "You've been wanting to 'redo' the kitchen."

"There's paint all over the floor," Mrs. Castor said, erupting. "And you, and the chairs, and what on earth have you put on the wall?"

"Sunburst Yellow," Lucy said in a quivery voice. "I found it at the Put and Take along with lots of other lovely colors."

"But what on earth possessed you?" Mr. Castor said, twitching his head around as if he had a nervous tic.

"I was trying to make the best of things." Lucy struggled not to burst into tears. She took a deep breath. "I thought if I made the kitchen sunny like it used to be, then it might cheer you both up and you'd start feeling happy again and saying hello when I come home from school and stop snapping and acting all worried and stressy like Grandpa always did, and start reading me *The Hobbit* and paying me some attention."

"Oh, Lucy," Mr. and Mrs. Castor said together. But Lucy was already bolting past them, scurrying down the hall and up the stairs to her room. She buried herself deep in her mouse hole, forgetting that she was covered in bright yellow paint and smearing it all over her sheets.

15

LUCY WASN'T SURE IF SHE WOULD EVER COME out of her mouse hole again. Her parents would probably never forgive her. What had she been thinking? It had seemed like such a good idea at the time, but now whenever Lucy shut her eyes all she saw was Sunburst Yellow, and she let out soft wails of despair. It took a great deal of coaxing from her parents, who Lucy felt sure were still furious with her, even if they didn't sound mad, before she poked her head out of the covers.

"I am an extremely fragile mouse," Lucy whispered. "So please don't shout at me again."

"No one's going to shout," Mr. Castor replied, "but I

insist on carrying you into the bathroom and washing your feet off just in case there's any wet paint left on them."

Lucy did offer to help clean up the kitchen, but Mrs. Castor said "no" rather firmly, much to Lucy's relief. She couldn't bear looking at the mess she'd created, because it would make her feel sad all over again. Understanding that their daughter was still feeling delicate, Mrs. Castor brought Lucy a bowl of cereal out to the hallway, and she ate it sitting on the stairs, watched over by the comforting face of the grandfather clock.

"I don't think I feel up for school today," Lucy announced to her parents. "This has not been at all the sort of morning I had hoped for."

"No, it took us all by surprise," Mrs. Castor remarked, "and I have a lot to do today. I've got a doctor's appointment and . . ."

"You have to clean up my mess," Lucy added with a sigh. Then rather wistfully she said, "I was just trying to brighten things up around here and make everyone happy again."

"I know, Lucy," Mr. Castor said, handing Lucy her school bag. "Come on, we're both late for school as it is."

"Are you going to put me up for adoption because of this?"

"I think we'll keep you around a little longer!" he said cheerfully, but Lucy couldn't help wondering if he were joking. Perhaps when the new baby was born they wouldn't want her anymore.

"Well, I think painting the kitchen was a lovely idea," Rachel said at recess. "That's so sad your parents didn't like it." The girls were huddled under the maple tree as usual, sharing Lucy's rather stale crackers, because Rachel's mother had forgotten to pack Rachel a snack, when Ella and the sparkle girls came hip-hopping over.

"How's your mom doing?" Ella said, twirling around and doing a fancy shuffle thing with her feet.

"She has a doctor's appointment," Lucy answered rather glumly, trying not to make eye contact with Ella's bright yellow shirt.

"Ohhh, fun!" Ella clapped her hands. "Is she going to find out whether it's a boy or a girl? I hope it's a girl, I really do. There's this tiny little girl in our dance troupe. Right, Summer? She can't be more than four."

"She's three," Summer said. "And she is soooooooo cute!"

"Why do you look so miserable?" Ella asked, noticing Lucy's expression.

For a moment Lucy didn't know what to say. Her ears grew warm, but Ella looked so concerned, Lucy said, "I painted the kitchen yellow and my parents got really mad."

"It was meant to be a nice surprise for them," Rachel added in her soft voice.

"But your kitchen would look adorable yellow," Ella said. "Did they get really mad? I can't imagine either of your parents getting cross."

A soccer ball rolled toward them, and Lucy watched Thomas and Jarmal chase after it.

"Put it this way. My dad shouted." Lucy cringed as she thought about what she'd done. "And he is not usually a shouter."

"Why did your dad shout?" Thomas panted, beating Jarmal to the ball.

"Lucy painted the kitchen as a surprise for her parents," Ella explained, giving her ponytail a flip. "Wasn't that sweet?"

"Wow!" Thomas shook his head. "Wow!" he said again. "You must be in so much trouble, Lucy. My mom and dad would ground me for life if I did anything like that."

"One time my brother scribbled on the wall with his crayons," Jarmal told them. "I've never seen my mom so angry."

"This was different," Rachel said. "Lucy was trying to be helpful."

"That's what my brother said. Apparently, he was 'decorating' the kitchen," Jarmal told them with a grin. "He still got no screen time for a week."

When the bell rang after the last lesson, Lucy stuffed her spelling words into her backpack and trudged into the hall with Rachel. If there were a bus going to Australia parked out front, she would most certainly be getting on it. She could hear the sparkle girls talking behind them about their Halloween costumes. They were going as the Jewels, an all-girl rock band that Lucy hadn't even heard of. Since there were five members in the band, May had asked Shawna to be the drummer, and Shawna was telling them how she planned to borrow her brother's drumsticks and leather jacket.

"And my mom is buying matching sparkly headbands for us all to wear," Ella said. "Just like the Jewels."

Lucy's stomach had started to ache. "Are you going trick-or-treating?" she asked Rachel softly. "Because you can come with me if you like. That is, if you don't have someone to go with already."

"Seriously?" Rachel beamed at Lucy, her eyes looking all sparkly and catlike behind her glasses. "I'd love to. I usually end up having to go with my dad and my annoying little brother. Which is not exactly fun," Rachel admitted, "because my brother always wants to go home before me so I never get that much candy."

"Do you know what you're dressing up as?"

"I was thinking either Arwen, my favorite elf princess, or some sort of Hungarian gypsy person who plays the accordion."

"Go as Arwen," Lucy said quickly. "Elf princesses are the best. I went as one last year," she added, not mentioning that Ella had gone as one too. "I'm not sure what I'm going to go as yet. Maybe a gnome," Lucy whispered.

"Hey, no running," Mr. Pritchard, the gym teacher, yelled as Michael Taylor came barreling out of the sixth-grade classroom and knocked Lucy straight to the floor.

"Sorry," Michael said, putting out a hand to pull her up. "I didn't see you. I'm so sorry."

"That's okay." Lucy struggled to her feet. She gave her arm a rub and smiled to show there were no hard feelings.

"Here." Michael picked up Lucy's backpack, tucking in the pencil box that had fallen out of the side pocket.

"Wait, Lucy, this fell out too," May said, and turning around Lucy saw May picking up her notebook. A hot wave of panic washed over her, but it was too late. The book had fallen open on the page with her gnome drawing. "Oh, how cute," May squealed. "A little elf, Lucy!" The girls started giggling, and Lucy tried to grab the notebook.

"Give that back—it's mine."

"In a sec. He's adorable!" May held the book up high. "*Magical Signs*!" she read as Summer, Shawna, and Molly crowded around. "*One. Seeing a gnome in my cupboard. Two. Finding sparkles from the gnome's shoes on my cupboard floor.*"

"Give that back," Lucy begged, feeling sick and dizzy. Her face throbbed with heat. "Please."

"Stop it," Ella snapped, tugging the book out of May's hands. "That's not funny, May, and it's not yours."

"Sorry." May looked uncomfortable. "I didn't mean it like that." She chewed at her thumbnail. "I thought it was meant to be funny."

Ella closed the book and gave it back to Lucy. "Are you okay?" she asked softly. Lucy nodded, holding the notebook tight against her chest. Her lip had started to quiver and she couldn't seem to stop it.

"I am sorry, Lucy," May said.

"She didn't mean to be mean," Ella whispered, giving Lucy a hug.

"I know," Lucy croaked around the lump in her throat. She managed a faint smile. But there was one thing she had no intention of being for Halloween anymore. And that was a gnome with sparkly, curly-toed shoes.

16

RACHEL HAD OFFERED TO WALK HOME WITH Lucy, even though her house was in the opposite direction and she was carrying her accordion case. "That's very nice of you, Rachel," Lucy said, standing outside the school gates. "But I don't feel like talking right now."

"We can walk in silence," Rachel suggested. "I don't mind silence. In fact I'm really good at silence. I've had a ton of practice. Or I can tell you a story about when we lived in Georgia and a hurricane blew away our garden shed. You wouldn't have to say a word."

"Thanks for the offer, but I couldn't concentrate on anything right now," Lucy said. "I'm not sure how mad my parents are going to be." She winced at the memory of this morning. "And I probably couldn't invite you in for milk and cookies, so it's better if I walk by myself."

"Well, I'm super happy we're going trick-or-treating together on Friday," Rachel said. "And if you need a long white beard for your gnome costume, we have one in our dressing up trunk you can borrow."

Lucy shook her head vigorously. "Do you have any long brown tails in your trunk? Because I've decided to go as a mouse."

The closer Lucy got toward home, the slower she walked, shuffling through great piles of leaves. It was Chloe who met her at the door. She could see her parents hovering in the hallway. "Put these on," Chloe said, handing Lucy a pair of rhinestone studded sunglasses.

"What are they for?" Lucy asked suspiciously. She glanced at her mother. "What's happening, Mom? And why is Dad home?"

"I went with your mother to her doctor's appointment," Mr. Castor said. "Now do what Chloe says and put the glasses on, please. Trust me, Lucy. You're going to need them."

"Hurry up, Lucy." Chloe clapped her hands.

Lucy sighed and did as she was told. "I'm not in the mood for silliness," she told them.

"Come on." Chloe took Lucy by the hand and led her

through to the kitchen, her parents following behind. There were still dishes on the table and a basket of laundry sitting on a chair, but no lemon-colored drips or smudgy yellow footsteps speckled across the floor. "Ta-da!" Chloe said, gesturing at the wall. Lucy turned and looked. She stood quite still, staring.

"Well, what do you think?" Mrs. Castor said after a few moments. "Didn't Chloe do a wonderful job? It was all her idea."

"I think . . ." Lucy sighed, gazing at the beautiful yellow sun Chloe had managed to create from Lucy's mess. "I think that it's absolutely, positively perfect."

"You did most of it, Lucy," Chloe said. "All I did was even out the edges, make the points a little more defined."

"It's glorious," Lucy breathed, stepping closer. "It's magic, Chloe!" This was nothing like the splotchy yellow disaster she had left that morning. The paint had been smoothed out so there were no brush marks visible, and it was just like having a big, beautiful sun lighting up the kitchen. "You're the best, Chloe."

"We're not done yet," Chloe said, turning Lucy toward the window and sliding off the rhinestone sunglasses. "Look outside."

"Oh gosh!" Lucy gasped, bursting out laughing. "Oh, Chloe, I just love it." Mrs. Minor's fence now had two big tubs of petunias painted on it—bold, beautiful petunias in a riot of crazy colors that Lucy recognized at once. There was Shock Your Socks Off Green, Purple Explosion, Electric Pink, Groovy Orange, Zoom to the Moon Blue, and a smidgen of Sunburst Yellow. "You did that?"

Chloe shrugged, looking slightly embarrassed. "It didn't take long, and I love to paint."

"Your dad and Chloe went back to the Put and Take and nabbed the rest of the paint before anyone else took it," Mrs. Castor said.

"But why?" Lucy questioned, studying her mother. She had an uneasy feeling something else was going on, but she couldn't put her finger on what that something else might be.

"Because you're right, Lucy," Mrs. Castor said, rubbing a hand across her belly. "Things have been gloomy around here lately. I haven't been feeling well and your dad's been worrying a lot. But you reminded us that life is actually pretty wonderful and we have a lot to be happy about." Mrs. Castor glanced at her husband, and the uneasy feeling inside Lucy grew. "Now every time we look at the fence, we'll remember the petunia moments and not all the yucky stuff."

"So let's have a picnic tea in the garden," Mr. Castor suggested, which made Lucy smile because only her dad would suggest a picnic outside at the end of October. "It's not that cold out there." Lucy saw her mother raise her eyebrows. "Okay, it's a little on the cool side," Mr. Castor added. "But we can bundle up in our coats. It'll probably be the last picnic of the season."

"Right, I'm off," Chloe said hastily, giving Lucy a quick hug. "Glad you like it."

"Wait, Chloe gets to stay too, right?" Lucy said. "You can't do all that work and not stay for the picnic."

"Mel and Jack are coming over," Chloe said. "Plus, I think this is a special sort of family picnic, Lucy." And before Lucy could ask her again, Chloe had already left.

The cake wasn't homemade, but it was chocolate and it was delicious. Lucy ate three slices, scattering crumbs down her thick wool sweater. She was just thinking about a fourth slice when Mrs. Castor cleared her throat in the way grown-ups do before they make an announcement.

"So, Lucy, remember how you were saying prime numbers were so special? How you didn't like four because it was all boring and common?"

Lucy looked at her mother, the uneasy feeling returning. She wasn't sure where this conversation was going, but something about it made her extremely nervous.

"Why are we talking about prime numbers?" said Lucy, her mouth going dry.

Her parents glanced at each other again. "Because we're going to be a family of five, not four," Mrs. Castor said.

"Oh, you're getting me a dog!" Lucy squealed. "A proper pet. I knew something else was going on. I could just tell by your faces, and you kept giving each other those looks."

"Lucy," Mrs. Castor said.

"Can we have a yellow Lab? I know they're big dogs, but they make the best companions. Or a golden retriever or a Great Dane?"

"Lucy," Mr. Castor said. "Calm down a minute. We're not talking about getting a dog."

"We're not?" Lucy said, her excitement fizzling away. "What are we talking about then?"

Mrs. Castor rested her hands on her belly and smiled. She looked bigger than usual, but that was probably because she was wearing her puffy down coat. "We're having twins."

"Twins?" Lucy repeated. Even though she knew what twins were, she could not quite believe what she was hearing. "Twins," she said again.

"That's what the doctor told us this morning," Mrs. Castor explained. "That's why I've been feeling so sick."

Lucy stared at her parents, but no words came out of her mouth.

"Aren't you pleased?" Mr. Castor said, slipping an arm around his wife. "Twins, Lucy. Can you believe it?"

Lucy nodded, but she still couldn't speak.

"It's certainly going to get a little louder around here," Mrs. Castor said.

"We'll be just like the O'Briens," Mr. Castor joked,

which Lucy did not find the least bit funny. "A houseful of screaming toddlers!"

Mrs. Castor glanced at the fence. "Poor Mrs. Minor. She's not going to like all the extra noise."

"Aren't you excited, Lucy?" Mr. Castor said.

Her parents clearly were, and Lucy hated to disappoint them. Especially since they had let Chloe paint petunias on the fence and cleaned up all Lucy's mess.

"It's great," Lucy finally managed to reply, trying her hardest not to burst into tears.

17

THE NEXT DAY IN SCHOOL LUCY COULDN'T think about anything else. It was impossible to concentrate, and as soon as morning meeting was over with and the bell rang for recess, she hurried along to the music room to wait for Rachel, who was having a makeup accordion lesson with Ms. Larkin. Through the window Lucy could see Rachel, playing away, but the noise leaking into the corridor sounded like a herd of dying cows. Worse than a herd of dying cows. This couldn't possibly be what polka music was meant to sound like, and Lucy wished Rachel hadn't spotted her because now she would have to think of something nice to say. Although she needn't have worried because as soon as Rachel came out, she took one look at Lucy's face and said, "Okay, what's the matter? I wasn't that bad was I? You look like you've just been tortured."

Lucy attempted a wobbly smile. "I found out last night. My mom is having twins. It's just a bit of a shock, that's all. So many new people in the family." And then before she could help herself, tears were leaking out of her eyes.

Rachel didn't say anything, just held out a bag of Cheez Doodles. "Thank you," Lucy said, helping herself to a few. She sucked on the cheesy, salty puffs, realizing that this was exactly what she felt like eating right now. It was amazing, Lucy thought, how telling Rachel her news and sharing her Cheez Doodles had managed to cheer her up.

On their way back to class they were stopped by Ella and May in the corridor. "I'm sorry about yesterday," May said, glancing at Lucy. "I just didn't think you were serious about all that gnome stuff."

"It's fine." Lucy shrugged, her eyes still a little red and watery.

"Lucy, what's wrong?" Ella said. "You've been crying. What's the matter? You're not still upset with May, are you?"

There was no point in keeping it a secret, Lucy realized. Everyone was bound to know sooner or later. "My mom feels really unwell," Lucy said, as if this were the reason for her tears. "She went to the doctor's yesterday, and they told her she's been feeling so sick because she's going to have twins."

"Twins!" Ella squealed, jumping up and down. "You are so lucky, Lucy." Lucy was beginning to feel quite worried. Maybe she lacked some big sisterly gene or something.

"Please don't tell anyone yet though. I know people are going to find out, but I'd like to try and keep it quiet for a bit."

"Course," Ella said, and May nodded in agreement. "We won't say a word."

By lunchtime, most of Lucy's grade and a couple of the teachers seemed to have heard that Lucy's mother was expecting twins.

Thomas and Jarmal made straight for Lucy and Rachel's table in the cafeteria. "Twins are the worst," Thomas said right away, unpacking his lunch.

Rachel shot him a warning look. "That does not help. Okay, Thomas?"

"I'm just being honest," Thomas said. He took a big bite of cheese sandwich and carried on talking as he chewed. "My aunt had twins, and as soon as they were born she started ignoring my oldest cousin. Completely. Lost all interest in him. She even stopped going to his soccer games and told him to hush every time he opened his mouth. And," Thomas added in a somber tone, "she forgot his packed lunch for weeks in a row. It made Adam so miserable he ran away."

"You are making that up," Rachel said. "Take no notice of him, Lucy."

"It's the truth," Thomas replied. "They're so spoiled, those twins. Get whatever they want and Adam gets nothing."

"How long did he run away for?" Lucy asked in an anxious voice. "Weren't his parents worried? Didn't they miss him?"

"To be honest I don't think they even knew he had gone. It was days and days before they realized he hadn't been coming to the dinner table. Poor Adam." Thomas sighed, finishing up his sandwich. "It's a bit better now but not much. He has to sleep in the attic where it's all dusty and full of spiders, and the twins got his room."

"Thomas, put a great big sock in your mouth," Rachel snapped, sounding most un-Rachel-like. "I don't believe a word of that."

Lucy had been dreading Halloween without Ella, but it turned into one of those lovely surprises, which are even more wonderful because you don't see them coming. Chloe had made Lucy a mouse suit out of the remains of the brown velvet curtains. It was as soft and snuggly as a pair of flannel pajamas. She sewed on a long stuffed tail and made a pair of large mouse ears that covered up Lucy's own mouse ears nicely.

"Perfect," Lucy squeaked, scurrying around the room. Rachel came over early, and the girls carved pumpkins and ate donuts and apple cider, and then Chloe and Mel took them out trick-or-treating. Lucy wasn't sure if she wanted Mel to come, even though Mel had dressed up in a pink tutu with bells around her ankles. But she kept twirling around, saying she was Tinker Bell, and Lucy and Rachel couldn't help laughing, especially when Mel scattered pixie dust over their heads. And after visiting a few houses Lucy realized she was glad to have Mel with them. Mr. Castor had to stay and be on door duty, because Mrs. Castor was curled up in the Nest with Mildred.

At one point the O'Brien boys surged past. They were all dressed as superheroes, jumping ahead of Mr. O'Brien in a karate kicking pack. Even Toady had joined in, wearing a wooly Batman hat and little cape, bouncing up and down in his baby carrier.

Although the streets were crowded with trick-or-treaters, it was hard to miss the sparkle girls, racing around with their cardboard instruments and sparkly headbands. They didn't have a grown-up with them, but Lucy wouldn't have wanted to go without Chloe or her dad. There was something genuinely scary about all those masked faces and ghouls, and Lucy was glad to have Chloe nearby. She was also glad to be going with Rachel, who made a magical elf princess. The last door they knocked on was Mrs. Minor's. She didn't have any pumpkin lanterns on her porch, but there was a faint glow of light coming from the front room, even though the curtains were drawn.

Lucy could feel her palms sweating as they banged on the door, deliciously terrified that Mrs. Minor might actually answer. She had images of being hauled inside and locked in a cage while Mrs. Minor stuffed them full of candy until they were plump enough to eat. Glancing over her shoulder Lucy was relieved to see Chloe and Mel waiting for them on the street.

"She's watching television in the dark," Rachel whispered, peering through a crack in the curtains. "That's so sad."

"Why is it sad?" Lucy hissed. "Mrs. Minor is an evil fence putter-upper."

"I bet she's lonely," Rachel whispered. "Imagine sitting there all by yourself with no family and no friends. People Mrs. Minor's age should have grandchildren running around. And she probably finds all the big kids in those horrible masks scary. I know my gran does."

"Now you're making me feel sorry for her," Lucy whispered, her eyes glued to the gap in the curtains. This was a new feeling and quite unexpected, but Rachel was right. There was something sad about Mrs. Minor, sitting all by herself on Halloween. *That could have been me,* Lucy thought dramatically. *Sitting all by myself, feeling sad about Ella.*

She impulsively slipped a mini bar of chocolate under the door, hoping this might make Mrs. Minor realize she had friends, and then maybe her frozen old heart would thaw a little bit and she'd take down that ugly fence.

18

LUCY FOUND IT STRANGE THE WAY HER MOTHER'S belly started to grow. It was as if she had swallowed a watermelon and then a beach ball, and still Mrs. Castor kept expanding. The house overflowed with stacks of hand-me-down baby clothes and brightly colored plastic toys, dropped off by the Castors' friends. "Perhaps some of these things can go to the Put and Take?" Lucy suggested, stepping on a set of plastic keys. "We can't possibly need all this stuff."

One afternoon Mrs. O'Brien stopped by with a bag of Toady's old baby clothes, and Mrs. Castor had invited her to stay for a cup of tea. This would have been fine if she hadn't brought all the boys along too. Lucy had been enjoying some quiet coloring time at the kitchen table, and now Micky was pressing too hard with her markers, ruining the ends, and Billy was sitting on his book, in case anyone tried to steal it, he had informed them. Although who in their right mind would want to steal such a disgusting soggy thing, Lucy couldn't imagine.

It took all her willpower not to say anything as she watched Billy waste her special paper, scribbling circles and grabbing another piece before he had even finished filling up the first sheet. Sammy was drawing superheroes with her favorite purple pen, and the Toad was flopped across Mrs. O'Brien, drooling and crying and making Lucy's head ache.

"He gets terrible tummy aches," Mrs. O'Brien said as she jiggled Toady up and down. "All windy and gassy, poor boy."

Trying to ignore the commotion (and Toady's windy, gassy smell), Lucy focused on her picture of a magical wood she was drawing. She carefully sketched a staircase inside one of the trees, which ended in a doorway leading to the cupboard in her room. Lucy had decided this was how her gnome got in and out. Whenever he heard her opening the door, he slipped out through the back of the cupboard to his gnome wood, except that one time, of course, after vacation, when she had taken him by surprise. *He probably got lazy and thought we had moved away*, Lucy mused, coloring in her gnome on the stairs.

"It's so much fun having a large family," Mrs. O'Brien was saying, although, for the life of her, Lucy couldn't understand where the fun part came in.

"I need purple," Micky said, trying to grab the marker away from Sammy and knocking over his cup of milk. Before Lucy had time to react, it had spilled across the table, soaking her picture into a wet mess. She watched her wood disappear in a flood of watery colors.

"At least it wasn't hot tea," Mrs. Castor said, lurching to her feet. "No one burnt, thank goodness."

"Oh, Lucy," Mrs. O'Brien murmured, noticing Lucy's drawing. "I'm so sorry. Your beautiful picture. Say sorry, Micky."

"Sorry," Micky parroted.

Lucy could feel milk dripping onto her favorite pants. She stood up and said rather softly, "I think I'm going to go outside."

"Me too, me too," Micky chattered, flinging down his pen.

"No! You can't," Lucy snapped, not caring if she sounded rude and wishing the O'Briens lived somewhere very far away.

"I'm really sorry, Lucy," Mrs. O'Brien called after her.

"It's okay," Lucy said, slipping out the back door. But it wasn't okay at all. She stood for a moment, shivering in the cold, before walking over to Mrs. Minor's fence and giving it a fierce kick. The hardest kick she could manage.

"Hey, I saw that," Chloe called out, and Lucy turned with a start. She hadn't realized Chloe was outside, sorting through the recycling.

"You won't tell my parents, will you?" Lucy said, her big toe throbbing as she hurried over. "I didn't break it."

"That doesn't make it all right, Lucy. You could easily have cracked one of the boards."

"Well, it's not like the police are going to arrest me for kicking a fence," Lucy said, immediately regretting her words. Chloe's face flushed as pink as her hair.

"You're right. But it's still not okay." Chloe looked down for a moment and then back at Lucy. "Look, I know what it's like to be mad, all right. When my parents were getting divorced, I was furious. I hated the way they argued all the time and I hated that my dad was moving out." She paused for a moment. "So one day, I went into Bella's Boutique, and I stole a pair of earrings and a scarf."

"You did?" Lucy stared at Chloe.

"Well, I tried to. Obviously, I wasn't a very good thief, because the manager stopped me and called the police. I ended up riding home in a police car. Which gave everyone in Hawthorne something to talk about!" Chloe gave a wry smile, and Lucy couldn't help feeling bad, remembering how she used to view Chloe. "The point is, Lucy. It's okay to feel mad, but there are better ways to deal with your anger than stealing stuff and kicking fences."

"It's not just the babies," Lucy said, her throat swelling up. "Or that Micky ruined my picture." She looked away and brushed a sleeve across her eyes. "Everything's changing and I can't stop it."

"Like what?" Chloe gently pressed. "Because change can be a good thing, Lucy, even if it all feels kind of terrifying right now."

"What if Rachel becomes a sparkle girl this summer, and I'm left behind without anyone to believe in magic with?" Lucy pulled a crumpled tissue out of her pocket and blew her nose. "I don't want to go into fifth grade, Chloe. Maybe I'll have to become a sparkle girl too and start listening to the Jewels and taking hip-hop." Lucy shuddered. "And that is just not me."

"It's not me, either," Chloe said. She laughed and wiped her hands on her jeans. "The nice thing is once you figure out all you've got to be is yourself, life is going to get a whole lot easier, Lucy. Now go and tell your parents you're coming with me on a Chloe adventure."

"What's a Chloe adventure?"

"You'll see," Chloe replied. "Just bring a coat and wear your boots, because we're going down to the river."

"To do what?"

"You'll see," Chloe said again. "And don't forget gloves."

A cold wind blew them along Beech Street. Lucy shivered inside her jacket, pulling on her gloves as they walked. This did not seem a particularly good idea, but she was interested to find out where Chloe was taking her. The Deerfield River ran along the west side of Hawthorne, and they cut across one of the many bike paths, weaving their way through a bank of trees and down to the wide, swollen river.

"Now, this is my special place," Chloe said, sounding serious. "I've never taken anyone here, and you have to promise me you won't tell your parents what I'm going to show you."

"Why? Is it dangerous?" Lucy said, starting to feel a touch nervous. "I'm not allowed to keep those kinds of secrets."

"There's nothing dangerous about this," Chloe said, picking her way along the riverbank. "But your dad would want to bring all his students here on a field trip and tell the newspaper and stuff. And what I'm about to show you is private." Chloe looked over at Lucy to make sure she understood.

"I promise I won't say a word, Chloe," Lucy reassured her. "And even though it's freezing cold and I'd love some hot chocolate, I'm so glad you are sharing your secret with me." This wasn't entirely true. Lucy had just slipped on a patch of rotting leaves, and the damp, earthy smell was making her nose run, but she didn't want to disappoint Chloe. Whatever Chloe was about to show her, Lucy would pretend to love.

"Careful going across here," Chloe instructed, pointing to a fallen log. In the middle of the river was a small island, and Lucy realized that Chloe expected her to walk across the tree trunk to get to it. It was a large log and didn't move when she stepped on top, but nevertheless she held her breath the whole way, not wanting to fall into the freezing water below. It was one thing going swimming in the summer, but quite another on a raw November afternoon.

"I used to come here all the time when my parents were fighting," Chloe said, crunching through the tangle of frozen undergrowth. On the far side of the island were a series of wide, flat rocks running into the river. Lucy followed Chloe, who had stopped beside a birch tree and was kicking leaves off the rock underneath. "Right there," Chloe said, nodding at the ground. "Isn't that amazing?"

"What is it?" Lucy asked, looking down. She crouched next to the flat stone and touched the shallow imprint of what appeared to be an enormous three-toed paw. "It looks like a footprint. But it's gigantic, like a dragon. Much too big for a bear or a moose."

"You're right." Chloe crouched beside her. "It's a dinosaur footprint. And no one else knows it's here. Not even Jack or Mel."

"How did you find it?" Lucy said, running both hands over the rock.

"By accident. I was sitting under this birch tree, feeling about as miserable as a person can feel, and when I looked down, there it was."

"Oh, Chloe, it's magnificent. It's so clear," Lucy whispered, tracing the outline of the footprint with a gloved finger. "He must have been an enormous dinosaur, like a *T. rex*."

"A *Eubrontes*," Chloe said. "An ancestor of *Tyrannosaurus rex*." She fiddled with one of her earrings. "I've been doing some research on the Web, comparing footprints found in this area, and I'm sure that's what it is." Lucy knew there used to be dinosaurs all over the valley. According to Mr. Castor this part of Massachusetts had been a big, hot swamp at one time, and when the dinosaurs walked across the mud flats they made footprints that hardened in the heat, eventually becoming rock that would last for millions of years.

"I can't believe it, Chloe," Lucy whispered. "A perfect secret footprint that no one else knows about."

"Ancient magic. That's what I call it," Chloe said, "because it's been here such a long time."

Lucy shivered with the thrill of such a find. "And you shared it with me."

"But you can't tell your parents."

"I won't tell anyone," Lucy promised, thinking that she

might need to sew her lips together to keep such a secret inside.

"The point is, Lucy, this footprint has been here for at least a hundred and ninety million years, but life keeps on going. It doesn't stop just because things change, and that's okay. That's the way it should be. There's no point in worrying about the future because it will happen, whether you like it or not, and it will probably be just fine."

Lucy nodded, staring at the enormous footprint and wondering if one of her footprints might still be around in 190 million years. But that was too big a thought to get her head around. She felt Chloe take her hand and give it a squeeze. Someone was burning brush on the other side of the river, and the air smelled of bonfires. A family of geese flew overhead, and right at that moment everything did indeed feel just fine.

19

MRS. CASTOR DIDN'T SAY ANYTHING TO LUCY about being rude to the O'Briens when they were visiting, but Lucy couldn't help feeling bad because she had snapped at Micky and run off by herself. Wanting to do something nice to make up for it, she decided to look through her spell book and see if there was anything in there which would cure Toady's stomachaches. Little bits of Sunburst Yellow were spattered across the cover, and Lucy picked them off with her fingernails, astonished by how far paint could travel!

"Gripe water for crying babies," Lucy murmured, studying one of the pages. It looked easy enough if she could find all the ingredients. "Chamomile, peppermint, fennel, ginger, caraway," Lucy read, running a finger down the list. She managed to unearth a box of chamomile tea from the kitchen and a rather dusty jar of crushed fennel seeds. There was plenty of fresh ginger root, which Mrs. Castor now bought by the bagful, but no caraway or peppermint.

"That plant on the kitchen windowsill is mint," Mrs. Castor said, giving Lucy a suspicious look when she asked her. "What exactly are you making, Lucy?"

"A little potion to stop Toady crying. Although I'm going to have to make it without the caraway," Lucy said, "but I don't think that will matter so long as I can come up with a good spell."

"Lucy, no," Mrs. Castor said firmly. "You can't go making up strange concoctions and giving them to babies to drink."

"Mom, it's a magic potion," Lucy insisted. "An all natural magic potion and I'm sure Mrs. O'Brien will love it."

"Lucy, is this really necessary?" Mrs. Castor said with a sigh as Lucy shook fennel seeds onto a cup of chamomile tea that still had the bag floating in it.

"I'm afraid it is."

"Then you are to tell Mrs. O'Brien exactly what you put in there," Lucy's mother said in her firmest voice. "I mean it, Lucy. You do not want to make Toady sick."

Mrs. O'Brien looked surprised and rather pleased when Lucy turned up at her door with a jelly jar of magic gripe water. "It's for Toady," Lucy explained. "To stop his tummy hurting."

"You made this?" Mrs. O'Brien said as Micky hugged his mother's legs and peered around them at Lucy. Sammy and Billy joined him, crowding in to see what Lucy had brought.

"I did. It's all natural," Lucy said, reeling off the list of ingredients. "But the most important part is the spell," she added, handing over the jar and a folded piece of paper. "You say it as Toady drinks the potion. It's the magic that really makes it work."

"I see," Mrs. O'Brien said, nodding. She held up the jelly jar, which was full of a murky-looking liquid with little flecks of leaves and seeds floating about in it. "Well, thank you, very much."

"Sounds like you should give him some now," Lucy suggested, hearing Toady start to howl from inside.

"What's the spell?" Sammy asked, staring up at Lucy.

Mrs. O'Brien unfolded the paper and read, "Toady, Toady, with a sore belly, you're a little bit loud, you're a little bit yelly. I can hear you screaming from across the road, so drink this potion and you'll be a happy toad."

"Funny," Micky said, starting to laugh.

"Funny," Billy repeated, speaking around the corner of his book he was sucking.

"It's not supposed to be funny," Lucy replied, a touch defensively. "It's magic."

"Well, this is very kind of you, Lucy," Mrs. O'Brien said. "I'm sure Toby will appreciate it."

"Toby?" Lucy said, looking puzzled.

Micky poked his head between his mother's legs. "When he was born, Billy couldn't say 'Toby.' He said 'Toady,' so that's what he's called."

"Oh," Lucy nodded. "Oh, I see. I thought it was . . ." She clamped a hand over her mouth. Clearly the Toad hadn't been called that because of his striking resemblance to one. Mumbling a hasty good-bye, Lucy dashed across the street before any more words came spurting out.

It wasn't until the weekend that Lucy discovered how her magic had worked. Mrs. Castor was taking one of her "never ending" naps, so Mr. Castor had suggested a walk in the woods, since it was such a mild December day. As Lucy stood on the sidewalk zipping up her jacket (not easy to do with a notebook wedged in the pocket), she watched Mr. and Mrs. O'Brien attempt to herd the boys inside their minivan.

"Your magic worked," Sammy shouted, catching sight of Lucy.

"Lucy's magic!" Micky shrieked, hopping about and doing some karate kicks.

"Come on, Dad, quick," Lucy said, tugging her father over. "Before they leave."

"It was amazing, Lucy," Mrs. O'Brien said as she buckled Toady into his car seat. "I didn't even need to give him the potion. Your spell worked just fine on its own."

Not wanting to be strapped down, Toady began to howl, and all three boys started yelling, "Toady, Toady, with a sore belly, you're a little bit noisy and a little bit smelly. I can hear you crying from across the road, so drink this potion and you'll be a happy Toad."

Toady immediately stopped fussing, broke into a gummy smile, and laughed.

"Works every time," Mrs. O'Brien remarked. "Honestly, Lucy, you're a genius."

"It's actually yelly, not smelly," Lucy explained. "The words do matter."

"Smelly, smelly," Micky chanted. "Toady is smelly."

"But I shouldn't think one tiny little word change would make that much difference," Lucy continued. "It is a very strong spell."

"I guess it must be," Mrs. O'Brien agreed. "Even worked in the middle of the night when Toady woke up crying."

"Lucy magic!" Billy chanted, clutching his book as Mr. O'Brien scooped him up and hoisted him into the van.

Lucy smiled shyly, and after the O'Briens had left, she slid her hand into her father's. "Do you really think it was the magic that made Toady stop crying?"

"Well, it's the only thing that seems to have worked," Mr. Castor said. He grinned at Lucy. "So yes, I would call that magic."

Pulling out her notebook, Lucy added the "stop Toady crying" spell to her list of magical signs. "They're actually not all that bad, those O'Briens," Lucy said. "Although I still don't want to babysit for them."

20

I'VE GOT AN APPOINTMENT AT THE HOSPITAL this afternoon for an ultrasound," Lucy's mother told her one Monday morning at the start of Lucy's Christmas vacation. "You can come with us if you like, or Aunty Karen says she'll watch you." Aunty Karen wasn't a real aunty, just a good friend of Lucy's mom's. She was also Lucy's godmother. "They're going to take pictures of the babies inside my belly," Mrs. Castor said with excitement, "and afterward we can go out for ice cream."

"Well, I'll definitely come if there's ice cream," Lucy agreed, thinking how much she loved the holidays. "And on the way home we can look at all the lights on the houses and give them marks out of ten for fanciness."

Mrs. Castor patted her stomach. "They'll be able to tell us what we're having," she said. "Boys or girls or one of each. Last time I had an ultrasound, the babies weren't very cooperative and we couldn't see!"

"I hope they're boys," Lucy announced rather quickly.

"You sound very definite about that, Lucy," her mom said. "I thought you would like a sister."

"Well, you have a girl already, so you don't need another. At least boys are a different species."

Mr. Castor laughed. "Boys are actually the same species, Lucy. We're all human."

Lucy wasn't sure she agreed with this. Not that it made a jot of difference. She still liked being the only girl in the family.

Snow had started to fall as they drove their way slowly to the hospital, a light powdered sugar coating that made Hawthorne look like a pretty picture postcard. This was rather unexpected because it hadn't been in the forecast. It was also the first snow of the season. Another sign, Lucy decided, because nothing was more magical than snow. Sliding down her window, she stuck her head out and let the cold flakes fly against her tongue. The air smelled of pine trees and wood smoke and Lucy laughed. This was her favorite time of the year and nothing could change that. She would get a large peppermint sundae with hot fudge sauce and crushed candy canes on top.

Inside the hospital it was warm and brightly lit. They waited in a room with a lot of other enormous moms. Lucy sat in between her parents, flipping through a fancy magazine called *Baking Delights*. She stopped at a picture of a three-dimensional coconut snowman cake with French meringue frosting and homemade caramel buttons.

"Oh, Mom, look at this," Lucy gushed, holding out the picture. "Can we make it?"

"Goodness!" Mrs. Castor stared at the recipe. "It requires three different sized cake pans and a candy ther-mometer."

"Yes, and we have to make a molded chocolate hat and spun sugar snow," Lucy pointed out. "Doesn't that sound fun?"

Just then Mrs. Castor's name was called, and Lucy's mom struggled to her feet, a little too eagerly, Lucy thought. "Better leave that magazine in the waiting room, Lucy," Mrs. Castor said. "Someone else might want to read it. We can have another look at the recipe on our way out."

Lucy and her parents were led into a small room where the sonogram would take place. A technician spread clear gooey jelly all over a long white probe while Mrs. Castor lay on a sort of bed. Her huge white stomach reminded Lucy of a giant balloon, the sticky out belly button looking just like the bit you tied a knot in. "Right now, Mrs. Castor, this will be cold," the technician said, rolling the probe across her mother's belly. She studied a computer screen beside the bed and tapped at some keys. "Mmmm," the technician murmured. "Let's see who we've got in here, shall we?"

Lucy suddenly felt sick. She wished she had not come. She wished she were safely at home in her mouse hole. She did not want to see who was in there at all.

"Baby one," the technician said, rolling the wand about. "And baby two."

"Oh, hello," her mother cooed, grasping Mr. Castor's hand. "Aren't they beautiful?" she said, starting to cry. "I'm sorry," Lucy's mother apologized. "I cry at everything these days."

Braving a look at the screen Lucy wondered if her mother were crying from joy or from absolute shock. She tilted her head to one side and then back the other way. "Are you positive those are babies?" Lucy finally said. "They look more like baby crocodiles with enormous egg heads."

"Two little girls," the technician replied, rolling the wand back and forth across Mrs. Castor's belly.

Lucy's stomach tightened. Her legs went all wobbly and she sat down on the edge of the bed. "Are you sure?" Lucy asked. "I have never seen a girl look like that."

"Quite sure," the technician said. "They don't have any, well, as far as I can tell, there are no . . ."

"No what?" Lucy said, puzzled.

"No little boy bits."

"What's a little boy bit?" Lucy asked, having no idea what the technician was talking about.

"You know, Lucy," Mrs. Castor said. "She means a . . ."

"Oh!" Lucy answered, staring at the screen. "Isn't that one?" she asked after a moment, pointing at a skinny waving thing.

"That's an arm, dear," the technician told her.

"Well, how about that?" Lucy said. "That's got to be one."

"That's a foot."

"I see." Lucy sighed, swinging her legs back and forth.

"And aren't they going to be lucky girls, having a big sister like you," the technician said. Lucy didn't answer. She just continued to swing her legs.

"Well, I say an ice cream celebration is in order," Mr. Castor announced, giving Lucy a hug. "Three little girls are exactly what this Castor family needs."

"Here, dear, you can have this," the technician said, handing Lucy a grainy black-and-white picture of the big-headed crocodiles. "Your two little sisters."

"Thank you," Lucy answered politely, thinking that three little girls were not at all what the Castor family needed. She followed her parents back through the waiting room, but her mother didn't stop to look at magazines. She had clearly forgotten all about the snowman cake, and when no one was looking, Lucy slid the sono-gram picture underneath *Baking Delights*.

The diner was crowded and Christmas music was playing as Lucy and her parents settled into one of the red vinyl booths by the window. It was Jack who brought over their ice creams, although it took Lucy a moment to recognize him, because he had smoothed down his spiky hair and taken the safety pin out of his ear.

"Two scoops of peppermint ice cream with hot fudge sauce and crushed candy canes," Jack announced with a grin, putting Lucy's sundae down in front of her. "I swirled extra whipped cream on there for you," he whispered, which was extremely nice of him, Lucy thought. The ice cream was delicious, but as she ate it she stared mournfully out the window, thinking about twin sisters and watching the snow turn into rain and wash away all the beautiful whiteness.

Lucy couldn't help wondering if she had been the one to make it happen, since she was feeling so miserable and weepy. Maybe she really did have magical powers. Maybe she could control the weather by her moods. Perhaps she had made it snow on the way over here because she had been feeling all Christmassy and festive, and now she had managed to turn the snow into rain with her sadness. Which meant, Lucy reasoned, with a spark of excitement, that if she started to feel happy again, the rain would stop? Putting her forehead against the window, she forced herself to smile. It wasn't an easy thing to do when you didn't feel the least bit like smiling, and Lucy watched her mouth in the glass, twisting into odd shapes. This made her smile for real because she looked so peculiar.

"Do you feel all right, Lucy?" Mrs. Castor said. "You're acting like you've got a brain freeze."

"I'm just extremely happy," Lucy said, thinking that some positive words of encouragement might make the sun come out. "I feel all sunny inside."

"Oh, I'm so pleased," Mrs. Castor gushed. "Honestly, you're going to love having sisters." She wrapped her arm around Lucy. "They're going to look up to you and think you're the most wonderful person in the world."

Thomas Blackburn walked into the diner with his parents. He shot Lucy a sympathetic look as they sat down at a nearby booth, and she gave him a little wave.

"So, Lucy, we've been thinking," Mr. Castor said, leaning across the table. "With two babies coming, we're going to need to come up with a different sleeping arrangement."

"I mean, they can sleep in our room for quite a while," Lucy's mom said. "But once they get bigger, they're going to need a room of their own, and it's just not fair to ask you to share with them both. One sister, maybe, but not two."

"What about the linen cupboard?" Lucy said. "We could

make it quite cozy for them. I'd help. We could paint it Sunburst Yellow, so it would be all bright and cheerful."

"That might be a touch small for two girls," Mrs. Castor said.

But not for two crocodiles, Lucy thought.

"So here's the plan," Mr. Castor said in a way too cheerful voice. "I'm going to move all the junk and stuff out of the attic and turn it into a special bedroom just for you. It's tucked away under the eaves, so it would be nice and quiet and give you some big-sister privacy. There are windows, and I'll put a proper floor down and carpet it to make it all nice and comfy." Mr. Castor stopped talking for a moment and glanced at Mrs. Castor.

"I'll make curtains for the windows, and we can pick out some pretty wallpaper," Mrs. Castor said.

"What do you think, Lucy?" her dad asked.

This was just what Thomas had warned her about. She was getting moved to the attic like his cousin Adam. The dusty, spider filled creepy attic. They'd forget all about her, hidden away up there, just like poor Cinderella. Lucy glanced at Thomas, who was digging into a huge meringue filled with whipped cream. He shook his head slowly, as if to say, *I told you so. This is what happens when twins come along.*

"I think it's never going to stop raining," Lucy said, pushing her sundae glass away.

21

CHRISTMAS CAME IN A FLURRY OF NOR'EASTERS. Mrs. Castor's stomach was now so big she looked as if she had eaten two whole turkeys. Usually Lucy and her parents all went tobogganing together, but this year Mrs. Castor stayed snuggled inside, engrossed in the baby sweaters she was knitting. She was too tired to make Christmas cookies with Lucy, let alone attempt a snowman cake. And she forgot to get *How the Grinch Stole Christmas!* out of the library. This was a ritual in the Castor household. They always read *The Grinch* over the holidays, but when Lucy's father dashed off to the library, every copy was already checked out.

It wasn't all bad though. Lucy did have Rachel over

twice for playdates. The girls made a rather successful memory cure for Mrs. Castor, who seemed to be forgetting everything these days, including where she had put the car keys. They stuffed a little cloth pouch full of dried rosemary (good for memory loss) and tucked one of Lucy's special handwritten spells inside. Then following the directions in *Nature's Magic*, Mrs. Castor placed the sachet under her pillow that night. Much to Lucy's delight, after breathing in the magical rosemary scent her mother actually remembered where she had put the car keys and that she had promised to make Lucy pancakes for breakfast!

The girls also turned Lucy's bedroom into an enchanted forest, which was easy enough to do, because it already looked rather forestlike and magical with all Lucy's nests. Plus, it was a great place to hide from the baby reminders scattered about the house. The one perfect petunia moment came when Chloe arrived the day before Christmas, bouncing with joy because she had been offered a place at Prachets next fall, and bearing a special gift for Lucy.

"Open it up now," Chloe said, the glass stud twinkling in her nose.

Lucy ripped off the paper and shook out a green dress decorated with delicate felt leaves. "My own elf princess dress," she screamed, jumping up and down. She held it up for her parents to admire. "It's just like yours, Chloe. I love it!"

That evening Lucy went through the ritual of hanging up her stocking and leaving cookies and milk out for Santa. Right before bed she snuck downstairs and grabbed a little butter cookie for her gnome, which she left on the floor of her cupboard. Lucy didn't mention this to her parents, because she had a feeling her mother wouldn't approve. She wasn't allowed to leave food lying around in her room, since most of the mice in Hawthorne seemed to know that the Castors' house was a lovely warm place to live in the winter. And Mr. Castor spent a great deal of time catching these furry visitors and releasing them outside again.

It was always difficult for Lucy to fall asleep on Christmas Eve, and she lay awake for a long time, listening for sounds against the thick, muffled quiet of the night. When a soft scratching broke the stillness, Lucy sat up in bed, holding her breath and staring through the dark at her cupboard. She imagined her gnome, crouched beneath her red sweater, munching away on the butter cookie.

"Merry Christmas," Lucy whispered, too scared to get out of bed and check. But first thing in the morning, she raced over to her closet, thrilled to discover that the cookie had indeed vanished. Lucy didn't tell her parents about this, because they might insist on putting a trap down, and what if her gnome got one of his curly-toed shoes caught in it? He would never come back again.

So she added *Gnomes like butter cookies* to her list of magical signs and then tucked the secret away in her head, next to Chloe's dinosaur footprint. Chloe's footprint was the first important secret Lucy had actually managed to keep. Secrets tended to leak out of her like juices bubbling from a pie, and Lucy had had to press her hands over her mouth many times to stop this one escaping. Much as she wanted to tell her dad about the footprint, she knew it wasn't her secret to share.

For the rest of vacation week Lucy wore her elf costume, spending most of her time in her enchanted forest bedroom. She rearranged her nests, drew a gnome village in her notebook, and gave her oil lamp a vigorous rubbing, just in case a genie should appear. Lucy already knew what she was going to wish for: a visit to Neverland with Peter Pan, so she wouldn't have to get any older. But however hard she rubbed, there was no genie, and she couldn't hide in her bedroom forever or stop school from starting up. And now they were deep into January, and it was impossible to keep on avoiding the fact that these babies would soon be here.

"Look what I found in the attic," Mr. Castor called out one morning, bumping something squeaky down the stairs. He had been up there since six o'clock—and on a school day! All this enthusiasm over moving Lucy out of her room was getting harder and harder to bear. Every time she walked into her bedroom now, she felt a pang of sadness.

She already missed her window seat, where she liked to snuggle up with a book, and the way the sunlight fell across her bed in the morning, as if waking her up with a smile. And what if her gnome came back again and she wasn't there to see him? It was hard for Lucy to truly believe her parents were going to force her to leave her cozy mouse nest for the attic. But judging from the piles of stuff being carted off to the Put and Take, this did seem to be the plan.

There was a creaking noise as her dad walked whatever his big discovery was along the hallway. "Remember Matilda?" he called through to the kitchen.

"Who's Matilda?" Lucy called back, carefully picking all the mushrooms out of her omelet. Her mother seemed to have forgotten that she didn't like mushrooms.

"This is Matilda," Mr. Castor said, wheeling a rusty, cobweb covered carriage into the kitchen. "She was your baby pram, Lucy. Don't you remember? You stayed in here till you were almost two. Refused to walk! We took you everywhere in Matilda."

"Oh, talking about baby prams, Aunty Karen is coming for tea," Mrs. Castor said, waddling over to the Nest. There wasn't even room for Mr. Castor on the sofa anymore, let alone Lucy. Mrs. Castor and the crocodiles took up the whole thing, and they still had two more months of growing to do.

"She wants to give us a new baby carriage as a present, which is lovely. We're going to look through some catalogs and find a nice double one. That way we can order it before she leaves for vacation tomorrow—ten days in California, lucky thing." Usually Lucy adored it when her mom's friend Karen came for tea, but lately all Aunty Karen wanted to do was talk about the babies. How she couldn't wait to see them and how she'd be over at their house all the time because Lucy's mom was going to need an extra set of hands.

"That's kind of Karen," Lucy's dad replied, and then turning to Lucy he said, "You know I'm making great progress clearing out the attic. I'm going to try and get it fixed up for you as soon as I can, Lucy. That way you can move in anytime."

"How nice," Lucy said, thinking that "nice" rhymed with "mice," and there'd probably be hundreds of them up in the attic. Still, she'd fit right in, and Lucy gave a long sigh, wondering if she'd ever feel like an elf princess again. She hadn't worn Chloe's Christmas present much lately, because it was hard to look like an elf princess on the outside when on the inside you were as small and inconspicuous as a mouse.

When Lucy got home from school that afternoon, she knew right away that Aunty Karen had arrived, because her car was parked out front. And when Lucy let herself in, loud Aunty Karen laughter could be heard coming from the kitchen. The banjo clock struck eight, even though it was only four, and a cuckoo clock followed right behind, the little carved bird flying in and out six times. It seemed as if all the clocks in the house were counting down the minutes until the babies' due date. Lucy could have sworn they were ticking faster and faster each day, as if time were literally flying. The problem was none of the clocks, except the grandfather clock and the station clock, told anything close to the right time, so it was a bit like living in a fun house with clocks striking crazy hours all day long.

Dropping her backpack on the floor, Lucy walked down the hall to the kitchen, her mother's voice drifting out to meet her.

"I just don't know what to do with her, Karen. I can't bear to part with her, I really can't. All those great memories." Lucy froze. She couldn't quite believe what she was hearing. Were they talking about her?

"But be honest," Aunty Karen said. "You don't need her anymore, do you? Not with a new shiny model coming along. And she's nine years old, don't forget. There's just not the room to keep her around, is there?" Lucy covered her mouth in horror. Thomas was absolutely right. Her parents didn't want her anymore. They were planning to get rid of their own child.

"So, any ideas who might want her?" Mrs. Castor was saying.

"Not really," Aunty Karen replied as Lucy doubled over with the shock. "Best bet would be to leave her at the Put and Take."

The Put and Take! Lucy's legs went all wobbly. She thought she might faint. What were her mother and Aunty Karen thinking? No parent would do such an awful thing, would they? Only in fairy tales where evil parents leave their children in the woods to get eaten by witches. But Lucy had heard them talking with her own mouse ears. There was no mistake. Or that's what it sounded like.

Her mother and father didn't want her anymore, and with a dramatic scream, loud enough to make sure her mother and Aunty Karen would hear, Lucy ran back down the hallway and out of the front door, slamming it loudly behind her.

She glanced over her shoulder as she sped along the street, to see if anyone were chasing after her, but neither her parents nor Aunty Karen were in sight. This made Lucy slow down for a moment. She couldn't believe they didn't want to come and find her, their own wonderful daughter. Well, she would run extremely far away and never come home again if that's how they felt. She'd find another family to live with. A family who would love a special elf princess and take care of her and treasure her and never ignore her or forget how special she was.

As Lucy ran past the Hawthorne railway station, she decided to go to New York. She'd live on the streets and join a band of orphans like Oliver Twist did. They must have orphans in New York as well as in London. She'd pick pockets and sleep in an abandoned house with someone called Fagin who would look after her. And one day her parents would take the crocodiles to New York to see a show, and they'd find Lucy begging on a street corner and be so happy to see her again that they'd burst into tears and promise her whatever she wanted if only she'd come home. It was such a satisfying daydream that Lucy didn't realize she'd walked right into the station and up to the ticket counter until the man behind the window said, "Where are you going, miss?"

"New York," Lucy told him in a confident, "I'm completely in charge of my destiny" sort of voice. "A one-way ticket, please."

"That's forty-five dollars," the man said, giving Lucy a hard look.

"Forty-five dollars! For a train ticket?" Lucy rooted around in her pockets. "I can give you forty-five cents," she said, putting some coins down on the counter. "Will that do? I am a small person," Lucy added, "and I don't take up much room."

"Are you her mother?" the man said, peering over Lucy's shoulder.

"No, I'm not," a woman replied, touching Lucy gently on the arm. "Do your parents know where you are, dear?"

"Because I can't sell you a ticket if you're by yourself. Even if you had the forty-five dollars," the man said.

An awful lot of eyes seemed to be staring at Lucy, and she felt her confidence evaporate away. "I have changed my mind," Lucy whispered. "New York is too dirty and noisy for me." Pulling away from the woman, she ran out of the station.

"You go right home," the ticket man yelled after her. "I'm sure your parents will be worried."

Lucy doubted that. She'd left home only ten minutes ago, and it didn't count as running away properly unless she'd been gone long enough for them to miss her. The problem was Lucy didn't know where to go. She hurried past the Candy Emporium on Main Street as a gaggle of schoolkids came bursting out, opening bags of jelly beans and caramels with their gloved hands.

"Hello, Lucy," Thomas said, offering her a caramel. Lucy glanced back at the station, to make sure the ticket man or the nice but nosy woman hadn't come after her.

"I'm running away," Lucy whispered, taking two caramels and putting them in her pocket in case she got hungry later.

"You are?" Thomas sounded a touch nervous.

Lucy sniffed, her nose red and dripping from the cold. "Well, your cousin Adam did, and I can see why now," she said, swallowing back her tears. "I am not wanted anymore."

"But, Lucy . . ." Thomas shuffled his feet.

"Where did he go?" Lucy asked. "Because I'm trying to decide myself. You said he was gone for days and days, and I'm wondering where he went."

"Well, not quite days and days. Certainly a few hours," Thomas waffled. "Definitely through lunch."

"So where did he run to?" Lucy said, eyeing the bag of caramels.

"The garden shed," Thomas admitted, looking rather worried. "But you should probably go home, Lucy."

"I don't have a home to go to," Lucy told him in her most pitiful voice. "I have been abandoned, Thomas. So if anyone asks where I am," she said, "I'll be at the Put and Take looking for a new family."

22

FOR THE FIRST TIME EVER LUCY DIDN'T FEEL
her usual excitement, pushing open the door of the Put
and Take. An old toaster sat on the table beside a stack of
paperback books and a heap of yellowish lacy fabric. The
books looked like the sort of thing Aunty Karen would
enjoy reading, with pictures of long-curly-haired women
on the front, bursting out of their dresses as they stared off
into the distance. On a different sort of day Lucy would
have brought them home as a surprise, but she didn't feel
like doing anything nice for Aunty Karen ever again.

There was a bench against one wall of the Put and Take,
and Lucy had to squeeze around a clunky metal file cabinet

and a rather rusty lawn mower to reach it. The file cabinet had been sitting at the Put and Take for months. No one seemed to want such an ugly piece of furniture, and Lucy knew just how it felt, all lonely and unloved.

As she wiggled past the cabinet, she yelped in pain, feeling a sharp jagged edge scrape the side of her leg. Blood started to drip down her shin, and she limped over to the bench, lowering herself onto the wooden seat. Lucy examined her leg and saw a long shallow gash. A slow burning sensation pulsed from the cut, and not having anything else to use, she took off her sock and pressed it against the wound. Drops of blood leaked out, white cotton soaking up the redness.

Lucy thought about going home, and then she thought about the conversation she had overheard between her mom and Aunty Karen, and although she couldn't really believe she wasn't wanted, big sad tears rolled down her cheeks, because that's what it felt like right now.

Why did everything have to change? The twins were going to get her special magical bedroom, and she was being forced into the attic. Lucy's tears started to fall harder. She didn't want to give up her gnome cupboard or her nest shelf.

It was quiet in the Put and Take, a dusty, lonely quiet and so cold Lucy could see her breath. She wondered how long she would be here before somebody found her. Every few seconds Lucy glanced at her watch, and exactly six minutes had ticked by when she noticed two boxes sticking out beneath the bench—boxes that hadn't been there on her last visit. Lucy stared at them for a while, until finally, unable to resist, she crouched down and pulled them out, wincing at the pain in her leg.

Obviously, someone had done a big attic clean out because both the boxes seemed to hold a jumble of old clothes, shoes, and books. At the bottom of one box was an antique cookie tin with a scratched flower design on the lid. Lucy tugged it out and sat back down, holding the tin in her lap. Getting the top off was difficult as the edges had rusted together, but with a lot of pulling and two broken fingernails she managed to remove the lid.

A folded letter lay on top of some scrunched up tissue paper. The letter was yellow with age, and when Lucy opened it up, the paper crackled like a dry winter leaf. "*December fifteenth, 1912*," Lucy whispered, which meant it had been written over a hundred years ago. *Dearest Clara*, she read.

> *Father and I send you our warmest regards and*
> *hope you are feeling better. I know boarding school*
> *is a big change and you have been missing home and*
> *feeling sad, but it is only a few more weeks until the*
> *Christmas holidays. We will be seeing you very soon.*

Lucy's hands started to tremble, as if the letter had been written just for her. She knew exactly how poor Clara must have felt, whoever Clara was. Taking a deep breath, Lucy read on.

Cook has promised to make a chicken pie on your first night back, which I hope will be something nice for you to think about.

I am sending you this little gift to remind you of your family and happy times. Do you remember the robin that made a nest in our pear tree? Well, I believe those naughty dogs from next door scared off poor mama bird, because we caught them barking and barking around the tree and she never came back to her eggs after that. We waited and waited, but there was no sign of her. Since it is such a pretty thing, Papa felt sure that you would enjoy having the nest at school. It was going to be a Christmas present, wrapped up under the tree, but we decided you were in need of a treat now. So here it is, darling Clara, and when you look at it you can remember your home and your family who love you very much and cannot wait to see you again.

From your ever devoted Mama and Papa

Very gently, Lucy lifted back the tissue paper to see what was underneath, and there, snuggled in the cookie tin, was a little robin's nest with three tiny blue eggs inside. "Oh, thank you," Lucy whispered, as if the gift had been meant just for her. "Thank you so much. I do feel better."

This was all the proof she needed. Magic did exist, and Lucy sat quite still, holding the tin on her lap as a warm buzz of happiness spread through her. When the door opened and Chloe walked in, Lucy still didn't move, not wanting to break the spell, scared that it might all vanish and she'd be left holding nothing.

Chloe bent over the table in her brown velvet cloak and picked up the piece of lace. She was wearing pink fingerless gloves that matched her pink hair and her pink, glittery nails. "Oh, I love this! An old tablecloth!" Chloe said, shaking it out. She looked up and gave a start, putting a hand to her chest. "Lucy! You scared the pants off me. What on earth are you doing here?"

"Look what I found," Lucy whispered, tilting the tin toward Chloe so she could see the nest. "This is magic, Chloe. And you have to read the letter that came with it. It's addressed to a girl called Clara, but I'm quite sure it's meant for me."

"Magic?" Chloe said, sitting down beside Lucy. She smelled of mothballs and spicy perfume. Carefully picking up the letter, Chloe began to read. When she had finished, she bent over the nest, lightly touching one of the robin's eggs with her finger.

"It has to be magic, don't you think?" Lucy said, studying Chloe's face and needing to hear her reply.

"Absolutely," Chloe agreed. "Remember what I told you? You just have to know where to look. Somehow this letter was meant to end up in your hands, Lucy. I do believe that."

"And it's working. I don't feel so sad about running away."

"Wait!" Chloe held up a hand. "You ran away?"

"My parents don't want me," Lucy said, although she didn't actually believe this anymore. "It was their idea to leave me at the Put and Take. So I came here to find a new home."

Chloe stared at Lucy and then she started laughing. "Oh, Lucy, you are funny."

"I don't see anything funny about my situation," Lucy said, remembering how upset she had felt. "There is nothing funny about not being wanted."

"But you don't really believe that. I know you don't. Your parents adore you."

"Well, I heard them say it with my own ears," Lucy told her. "There was no mistake."

"Whenever I used to run away, it was because I wanted attention," Chloe said gently. Not looking at Chloe, Lucy folded up the letter and placed it on top of the nest. She did want some attention. It felt as if she hadn't had any for a very long time. "Come on, Lucy, I'll take you home," Chloe said. She draped the lace tablecloth over her shoulder and held out her hand.

Lucy shook her head. "I think Clara's parents understand how I feel much better than my own parents," she whispered, taking the sock off her leg and wincing. "If they want me, they can come and get me." The cut was still dripping blood, and Lucy pressed the sticky sock back against it.

"Oh, that's nasty. What on earth did you do?"

"I cut it on the file cabinet," Lucy said with a wince. "And it really hurts."

"I bet it does." Chloe's voice softened. "You poor little thing."

"I've probably lost quite a bit of blood."

"You do need to get it cleaned. If there's rust in there, it could get infected."

"But I'm not ready to go home. I doubt I've even been missed yet."

"Then you can come back to my house," Chloe said rather firmly. "We'll clean you up there." She gave Lucy a serious look. "You do not want to get blood poisoning."

No, she did not, and Lucy leapt right up. She had read about blood poisoning in *The Book of Strange Facts*. If you didn't clean your wounds properly, you could end up with gangrene, and then you might have to get your limbs chopped off.

23

CHLOE'S PINK-GLOVED HAND WAS WARM AND soft and extremely nice to hold. In Lucy's other hand she carried the nest tin. As they crossed Main Street, Lucy saw Ella, May, Summer, and Molly heading off to dance practice in their matching fur trimmed boots. Under their open jackets they all wore pale blue sweatshirts with SUNSHINE STUDIO printed on the front, and had silver drawstring bags slung over their shoulders. Lucy noticed them glance over and then whisper to one another. Probably wondering what she was doing with weird Chloe, Lucy guessed. But she didn't care what they thought, and she didn't let go of Chloe's hand either.

"I'll call your parents first thing and tell them where you are," Chloe said, her velvet cape brushing against Lucy. "We don't want them to worry."

"Well, they can worry for a bit," Lucy said. "I'm okay with that."

In all the months Chloe had been working for the Castors, Lucy realized she had never been inside Chloe's house. She felt a little anxious, remembering the shouting she used to hear before Chloe's parents got divorced, but as soon as they walked in, Lucy relaxed. Chloe's mom was cooking in the kitchen, and there were laundry and books and the sort of usual clutter scattered everywhere that made a house feel like a home. The best part though was that there were no high chairs waiting to be assembled or bags of baby clothes waiting to be unpacked or plastic baby toys taking up all the floor space.

"Sit down," Chloe said, taking Lucy into the living room. "I'll phone your mom and dad and then we'll get that leg cleaned up." Chloe disappeared into the hallway, and Lucy sat on a sofa, enjoying having it all to herself. There was a lovely smell of frying onions coming from the kitchen. It made Lucy's stomach rumble, and she wondered what Chloe was having for her dinner.

"They'll be here shortly," Chloe said, coming back carrying a red first aid box. "I told them ten minutes, so that should give them enough time to miss you!" Chloe was smiling, and Lucy suddenly wanted to leave now. The onion smell was making her homesick, and she hoped her parents hadn't really been worrying. "Okay, let's get that cut washed," Chloe said, opening the first aid box. With swift, efficient strokes she cleaned Lucy's leg, doused it with antibiotic lotion, and put on an extra-wide, heavy-duty Band-Aid.

"What are you going to do with that tablecloth you took?" Lucy asked, trying not to squirm even though her cut stung.

"I'm going to make it into a shirt," Chloe said. "That's vintage lace someone's throwing out. It'll be beautiful once I've bleached it. I'll show you some of my designs if you like. I've got a whole book of them."

Lucy nodded politely. She did want to see some of Chloe's designs, but not right now. Right now it was time to go home. She had been gone long enough. Just then there was a knock at the door.

It was so nice to see her mother that Lucy almost forgot to be mad at her. But when Mrs. Castor gave Lucy a hug, it felt as if the babies were pushing her away. She couldn't get close to her mother because of her enormous belly. Mrs. Castor thanked Chloe for bringing Lucy back, and then taking her by the hand she led her daughter home.

Aunty Karen was in the kitchen making tea, and Lucy's dad was marking history tests at the table. The house smelled of lemon cake, which was even better than frying onions, but Lucy felt suddenly shy, remembering the conversation she had overhead between her mother and Aunty Karen. She stood in the doorway, clutching her cookie tin.

"What's in that beautiful box?" Mr. Castor asked, smiling up at Lucy. And then, in his quiet, serious voice he added, "We were worried about you, Lucy." He slid his fingers under his glasses and rubbed at his eyes.

"Oh, Dad, look what I found at the Put and Take," Lucy said, a gush of relief washing over her. This was her home and she had been missed. Just like Clara. She pried the lid off the cookie tin and handed her father the letter. "You can read it out loud, but please be careful. It's extremely old."

Lucy's parents and Aunty Karen were just as stunned as Lucy by the beautiful antique nest and the letter to Clara.

"What a special treasure for your collection," her father said. "And the eggs are in perfect condition. I'm surprised they haven't cracked."

"Clara obviously took great care of them," Lucy remarked. "Perhaps she collected nests like me." She gave a small, dramatic sigh. "I think we have a lot in common."

"Now, Lucy, what's all this about?" her mother asked gently. "Why on earth did you run off like that?"

"Because I heard what you said. I heard everything," Lucy told them, her anxiety returning. "All about not wanting me anymore because I'm an old model and how you were going to leave me at the Put and Take."

Mrs. Castor looked puzzled for a moment. "Wherever did you get that idea from?" And then she started smiling. "Oh, Lucy, we were talking about Matilda. Your old baby carriage! We're not going to need her anymore because Aunty Karen is giving us a lovely new double stroller. You didn't really think we'd leave you at the Put and Take, did you?" Lucy could tell Aunty Karen was trying not to laugh.

"Well, I have been extremely ignored lately," Lucy replied dramatically. "All you ever talk about are the babies. Even Aunty Karen seems more excited to see your belly than she is to see me. So yes, actually, it did seem very possible."

"Then we shall have to rectify that immediately," Mr. Castor said, "and have two chapters of *The Hobbit* later on."

"And you get the first slice of lemon cake," Aunty Karen said, putting a plate down in front of Lucy.

"And I'll make you some chocolate milk," Mrs. Castor offered, dropping a kiss on Lucy's head.

"Might I have a little more cake, please?" Lucy asked, enjoying all the lovely attention.

"Absolutely, Lucy," Aunty Karen said.

"And could you pass me my *Book of Strange Facts* to look at, please?"

"At your service, Lucy," her mother replied, waddling over with the book.

"And since we're on the subject of doing nice things for Lucy," Lucy said. "A new red ten-speed bike would be most appreciated."

"Right, and I'd like a new car and your mom wants a new laptop," Mr. Castor said.

"Well, it was worth a try," Lucy said with a grin.

When Lucy's parents came to tuck her in that night, they spent a long time admiring Clara's nest again. Lucy had placed it in the center of her shelf, and it was definitely her new favorite. Mr. and Mrs. Castor were now perched on either side of Lucy's bed, peering down at her with rather anxious faces.

"You have to be honest with us, Lucy," her mother said. "We want to know how you're feeling."

No, you don't, Lucy thought. *You don't at all.* She wondered if Clara had had any brothers and sisters. Maybe that's why her parents had sent her away to school, because of a new baby arriving.

"Life has been a little crazy around here lately," her father said. "Getting ready for the twins."

"And you are a bit excited, aren't you?" her mother asked. Lucy could see the crocodiles squirming about in her mom's belly. It seemed to Lucy as if they were thrashing each other with their tails. Her father was looking at her hopefully, and Lucy forced herself to smile.

"Of course I am," she replied, certain that her parents would never forgive her if they knew how she really felt inside.

24

AT SCHOOL THE NEXT DAY THOMAS LOOKED
extremely relieved to see Lucy. "So you didn't run
away for long, then?" he said, fiddling with something in
his pockets.

"Long enough," Lucy told him, narrowing her eyes.
"And I'm not sure I believe everything you've told me
about your cousin Adam."

"You shouldn't believe anything Thomas tells you,"
Rachel said, linking her arm through Lucy's.

Ms. Fisher was late coming to class, and Ella, Summer,
Molly, and May gathered around Lucy's desk while they

waited. "So what were you doing with that weird Chloe girl yesterday?" Summer asked.

"Yes, you were holding her hand!" May added, making a face.

"She's actually really nice," Lucy said. "I like her."

"She's been arrested by the police," Ella exclaimed. "My mom calls her a 'bad influence.'"

"Well, she's not. I was wrong about her," Lucy said.

"So do you know what she did?" Ella whispered. "Was it really awful?"

"Why don't you ask her?" Lucy said. "I'm sure she'd tell you."

"There is no way I'm talking to weird Chloe!" Ella replied as Ms. Fisher walked into the room.

"I don't really feel like eating in the cafeteria," Lucy said to Rachel as the girls dug their lunch boxes out of their backpacks after music class. "It's too noisy and full of people." The truth was Lucy didn't feel like sitting with Ella and the sparkle girls. They would pepper her with questions about Chloe, and the babies, and Lucy wasn't up for answering any of them today.

"Let's go back to the music room," Rachel said. "I'm sure Ms. Larkin won't mind. When I first came here I used to eat in the music room sometimes. I didn't know anybody and the cafeteria made me so nervous. I'd pretend I wanted to practice my accordion." Rachel smiled and took Lucy's arm. "Come on. I promise you, Ms. Larkin won't mind."

"Make sure you tidy up when you leave," Ms. Larkin said to the girls. "And try not to drop crumbs on the carpet."

The room was small and quiet and exactly where Lucy felt like eating. It was fun to eat lunch surrounded by trombones and drum sets and music stands. Lucy munched on a ham sandwich while Rachel ate noodles out of a thermos. That was the best thing about Rachel, Lucy thought. You could sit in comfortable silence with her and it never felt strained.

"Am I a bad person, do you think?" Lucy asked softly, opening up a vanilla yogurt and being extra careful not to drip on the floor. "Because I'm not looking forward to these babies coming."

"You're not a bad person at all," Rachel said. "I bet a lot of kids feel that way. I know I wouldn't really want my mom to have any more babies," she admitted. "One brother is quite enough. You can't help the way you feel, Lucy. But once the twins are here, it will be different."

"I really hope so," Lucy said with a sigh, wishing she felt as sure about this as Rachel did.

"Hey, I know what will cheer you up." Rachel jumped to her feet. "I'll play you the polka tune I'm learning."

"Oh, Rachel, you really don't have to do that," Lucy said,

but Rachel was already bounding over to her accordion case that was leaning against the wall.

"I want to. You'll love it. It's a happy song. And you'll be amazed by how much I've improved," Rachel added. She snapped open the case and took out her great-grandpa's accordion. The keys had yellowed with age, the engraving on the front was scratched, and there were chips in the black lacquered paint. It had clearly seen a lot of use over the years. "I don't know what this is called in Hungarian but in English Ms. Larkin says it means 'Run for the Hills.'"

Rachel started to play, pushing the bellows part in and out and pressing the keys at the same time. Her whole body was moving as if she couldn't keep still, and Lucy almost choked on her yogurt, staring in wonder as Rachel squeezed out a wheezing, off-key noise that sounded more like a stampede of mooing cows than a rousing polka. But at least these cows were mooing and not dying, like the last time Lucy had heard this particular tune. There was definitely a glimmer of improvement, and even though Lucy understood why it was called "Run for the Hills," she couldn't help smiling to see Rachel playing with such enthusiasm.

"Ms. Larkin says I'm really getting the hang of it," Rachel panted, finally coming to a stop. Her face was flushed as she looked at Lucy. "You feel better. I can tell."

"I do. I really do. That was"—Lucy's smile got broader as she searched for the right word—"that was unbelievable,

Rachel! And I could hear a difference. I really could."

"Seriously?" Rachel started to laugh which made Lucy join in. "Because I never said anything, but a few weeks ago I was beginning to think I might quit."

"Oh you can't, Rachel. I won't let you. You are getting better and you're the best cheerer-upper ever."

"And I do love how it makes me feel when I play," Rachel confessed. "All happy and bubbly inside."

"That's just how I feel when I find a new nest for my collection."

"I knew there was something else I wanted to tell you," Rachel said, putting her accordion back in the case. "This has nothing to do with polkas or nests but it's extremely interesting and I think you're going to love it." Walking over to Lucy she said, "Did you know that in the city of Grundarfjordur, the main street doesn't have a number 84? There's an 82 and an 86, but they're separated by this empty piece of land, which is where 84 should be."

This was such an out of the blue, Rachel thing to say, that Lucy felt a rush of affection toward her friend. "What are you talking about, Rachel, and where is Grundarfjordur?"

"Iceland, of course. I told you I've been reading up on the place. It's so fascinating. That's where Tolkien got some of his ideas for *The Hobbit* and *The Lord of the Rings* from."

"So why doesn't the main street have a number 84?" Lucy asked.

"You're not allowed to build on that lot. The land is protected because an elf lives there. At least that's what the town thinks. It's a special elf preserved plot."

"Really?" Lucy said, thinking what fun it would be to live at number 82 or 86.

"Cross my heart—it's completely true. I thought you'd like to know."

"It's the best thing I've heard all day," Lucy said. "Well the second best thing after your polka. In fact, when I grow up I think I might live in Iceland," she added. "I'm sure I'd have a lot in common with the people there."

When Lucy got home from school she found her mother napping in the Nest, looking, Lucy thought, like an enormous blue whale, dressed in a loose, pale blue smock thing. Her dad was already there because he had his free period at the end of the day on Wednesdays.

"Aunty Karen dropped off your favorite chicken casserole on her way to the airport," he said, trying to fix the clock that still wasn't fixed. He had found it at the Put and Take months ago. "And there are two more meals in the freezer," Mr. Castor continued.

"What if Mom has the babies while Aunty Karen is in California?" Lucy said, thinking that her mother's stomach couldn't possibly stretch any farther. "Who would take care of me while you're at the hospital?"

"Those babies have to cook for another seven weeks, Lucy. They're not nearly ready to come out yet. Aunty Karen is only going to be gone for ten days, so you don't need to worry about that."

Lucy watched her mother's stomach lurch over to the side as one of the crocodiles turned. Mrs. Castor opened her eyes and groaned. The groan turned into a smile when she saw Lucy looking at her. "Hello, Lucy. How was school?"

"Boring," Lucy said. "But I did learn some interesting things about Iceland from Rachel. It's a wonderful country, and I'm definitely going to live there when I'm older."

"They have very long, dark winters," Mr. Castor pointed out.

"They also believe in elves and dwarfs," Lucy said, giving her father a frosty stare. "Which is far more important."

"Absolutely," Mr. Castor agreed.

"And I also learned a few interesting things in my strange facts book during recess," Lucy continued. "I'm reading to Rachel now, since we've finished *The Lord of the Rings*."

"Sounds like you had a fact filled day," Mrs. Castor said with a yawn. "So what did you learn?"

"Some very cool stuff you can use in *Amazing Animals* if you like." Lucy was always trying to help her mom come up with unusual animal facts. "Did you know that an octopus will chew its arms off if it's under great stress?" she said.

"And an elephant's pregnancy lasts almost two years? Their babies weigh about two hundred and thirty pounds each."

"Glad I'm not an elephant," Mrs. Castor murmured, cradling her swollen belly. "Although I feel rather like one."

"I'm glad I'm not an octopus," Mr. Castor said, giving his arms a shake.

"Mom," Lucy blurted out. "What if you have the babies early?" This was beginning to worry her. "We're not nearly ready for them to show up yet."

"Well, they may come a little early, Lucy. Twins often do. But"—and Mrs. Castor gave her most reassuring smile—"it won't happen until Aunty Karen gets back from vacation."

25

FIVE NIGHTS LATER LUCY'S FATHER WOKE HER up. "Lucy," Mr. Castor whispered, the light from the hallway shining into the dark room. Lucy's eyes popped open at once. She sat bolt upright and stared at her father, all traces of sleep gone.

"Something terrible has happened," Lucy said, glancing at her alarm clock. It was half past one in the morning.

"Nothing terrible has happened, Lucy, but I didn't want you to wake up and find us not here."

"Is it Mom?" Lucy said, her heart thudding away at high speed. She covered her ears with her hands. "I can't bear to hear."

"Lucy, you mustn't worry," her dad said, using his extremely calm voice, which terrified Lucy even more. "Your mother's labor seems to have started, and I need to get her to the hospital."

"But it's too soon." Lucy panicked, feeling sick to her stomach. "The babies can't come now. They haven't finished growing."

"Lucy, Chloe is downstairs," her dad said. "She's going to stay with you because Aunty Karen's in California. We had to ask someone quickly, and she came right over. This way you can stay in your own bed. I have to go now," her father said, kissing Lucy on the forehead. "I'll be back as soon as I can."

"Look after Mom," Lucy whispered.

"Of course I will. And try not to worry."

Try not to worry? Lucy had never been more worried about anything in her life. She wanted to grab ahold of her father and hang on as tight as she could. She didn't want anything to happen to her mother. But she also knew she couldn't make a fuss. She had to be brave, even if she didn't feel at all brave inside.

Lucy heard whispered voices and then the front door banged shut. She lay quite still as she listened to the sound of a car starting up. In the quiet of the night it zoomed off down the street, heading straight to the

Hawthorne hospital. Reaching under her pillow, Lucy pulled out her old stuffed mouse. Hugging him tight, she screwed up her eyes, trying to fall back to sleep. But it was impossible. Terrible, frightening thoughts kept crawling into her mind, and she finally threw back the covers and got out of bed.

The lights were on in the hallway, and Lucy padded downstairs. She stroked the grandfather clock as she walked by, comforted by its soft, steady ticking. "Please keep my mom safe," Lucy whispered. "And the babies."

Chloe was sitting in one of the kitchen chairs, a jumble of lace in her lap. Lucy watched for a minute as Chloe sewed, making neat, tiny stitches with a needle.

"Did you know there's such a thing as a tailorbird?" Lucy said softly. "They sew with their beaks and use spider silk to stitch leaves together when they make their nests."

"Really?" Chloe looked up at Lucy. "Do you have one in your collection?"

"No." Lucy sighed. "They live in Asia."

"Maybe one day you'll go visit and you can bring one back," Chloe suggested.

Lucy shook her head. "I don't like being far from home." She had changed her mind about living in Iceland when she grew up. Her lip quivered. "I am not really a traveling sort of person."

Chloe nodded and kept on sewing.

"Aren't you tired?" Lucy asked. "It's the middle of the night."

"I'm a teenager," Chloe said. "We like to stay up all night. And eat junk food. And watch bad television."

"Well, I can't sleep," Lucy said, sighing. She didn't want to talk about what had just happened and the reason Chloe was sitting here, and she hoped Chloe wouldn't bring it up either.

"Would you like some hot chocolate?" Chloe offered. "That always makes me sleepy."

"Do you know how to make it?" Lucy said, thinking about Chloe's attempts in the kitchen.

"I'm sure I can figure it out." Chloe got to her feet and Lucy followed her over to the stove, looking out of the window as she passed. The pots of petunias painted on the fence glowed faintly neon in the darkness. Lucy wondered if the crocodiles would ever get to see them, or the sun Chloe had painted on the wall.

She didn't realize she was crying until she felt Chloe's arms wind around her. Lucy pressed her face against Chloe's sweater, the softness of the wool absorbing her tears. "Come on," Chloe said, leading Lucy over to the Nest. "You curl up here and I'll bring you some hot chocolate."

Chloe remembered to use Lucy's favorite I LOVE VERMONT mug although the chocolate wasn't quite hot enough. But Lucy didn't mind, and she felt suddenly sleepy as Chloe tucked a quilt around her.

"I'm glad you're here," Lucy murmured, watching Chloe sew. "Don't go to sleep before me, will you?"

"I told you, I'm a teenager."

"Chloe, can I ask you a question?" Lucy mumbled. "I keep forgetting to ask you, and I always think about it when you've gone home."

"Ask away," Chloe said, picking up her sewing.

"Why did you get an elephant tattooed on your leg? Why not a tiger or a lion, or another animal? And were your parents mad?"

"My parents were a bit mad, yes!" Chloe chuckled. She didn't say anything for a minute and then said, "When I got it, I felt invisible. I felt as small as a mouse, and I wanted to feel big and powerful like an elephant. So this reminds me to stay strong and rooted, even when life gets challenging."

"I'm a mouse," Lucy whispered. "A very small mouse. I wish I had my mouse," she mumbled. "But he's upstairs in my bed."

Lucy didn't hear Chloe leave the room, but she must have done, because at some point, half asleep, Lucy found her mouse tucked up beside her on the Nest.

26

WHEN LUCY WOKE UP CHLOE WAS SNORING softly in her chair. She still had her sewing in her lap, and Lucy realized she must have been sitting there all night. Her head had dropped forward and her pink hair hung over her face, making her look like a Raggedy Ann doll. Climbing off the sofa, Lucy walked over and gently covered Chloe with the quilt.

For a brief moment Lucy wondered if her parents had returned. Maybe they didn't want to wake Chloe or Lucy and were, at this very minute, tucked in bed upstairs. Maybe the hospital had given her mother some medicine to stop the babies from coming early and everything was all right again.

Lucy raced up the stairs and into her parents' room, but the bed was empty and the sheets were all crumpled and cold. Wandering out into the hallway Lucy noticed that the door to the attic was ajar. She hadn't been up there since her parents started cleaning it out, bringing down boxes and boxes of stuff to drop off at the Put and Take or leave at the town dump.

As soon as she opened the door Lucy smelled fresh paint. She hadn't realized her father had been painting up here. Switching on the light, Lucy climbed the narrow stairs. She kept her arms by her sides, scanning the steps for spiders, but it all appeared swept and clean. Not at all how Lucy remembered the attic looking.

When she got to the top step, Lucy stood for a moment, taking in her surroundings. Pretty cream-and-blue-striped curtains hung at all the windows, and the glass had been scrubbed until it sparkled. The space was light and airy. Instead of dirty, gray floorboards, the wide pine planks had been polished a warm shade of honey. There was even a blue-flowered rug that Lucy had seen at the Put and Take a few months ago. And running around the walls of the whole room, about five feet off the ground, was a long empty shelf that her father must have put up.

Sinking down on the floor, Lucy curled up into a ball and wrapped her arms around her legs. She rested her chin on her knees and started to sob, soft quiet cries at first that grew into big gusty wails. Lucy was so busy crying that she didn't hear footsteps creaking up the stairs. She didn't hear Chloe walk across the attic until she knelt down beside her.

"I always wanted Mom and Dad to do this to our attic," Chloe said. "What a lovely room."

"I know," Lucy blubbered, crying harder. "It's absolutely perfect. No spiders or cobwebs, and Dad even put up a shelf for my nests. I'm a mean, terrible person, Chloe. I do not deserve a room like this."

"That is the craziest thing I've ever heard!" Chloe put her arm around Lucy.

"This is all my fault," Lucy said. "I made those babies come early. I didn't want them here, Chloe. I wished they'd go away. And now they have, and Mom won't get to bring the crocodiles home and it's all my fault."

"Lucy, you had nothing to do with this. Bad thoughts do not make bad things happen," Chloe said. "And for the record, back in ninth grade when my parents were fighting all the time, I used to hate your family."

Lucy looked up, startled. "You did?"

"I really did. I wished you'd all move away. Your parents never yelled, and you were always having these picnics in the yard, and everyone seemed so happy all the time. I could tell they adored you and they adored each other, and

I used to feel so jealous that you had happy parents and I didn't. I couldn't even look at you."

Lucy wiped her nose on her sleeve. "I had no idea."

Chloe shrugged. "It's okay. Why would you? The funny thing is, my mom and dad are much better friends now they live apart!"

The girls sat in silence for a while, a nice, companionable silence, until the grandfather clock struck seven. "Do I have to go to school today?" Lucy asked. "I'm not at all in a school sort of mood. I think I should wait by the phone until my dad calls to tell me what's going on."

"Well, I think you should go to school and try not to worry," Chloe said. "And by the time you come home, I'm sure there will be news. Now, come on." She took Lucy's hand and pulled her to her feet. "I'm quite good at making oatmeal, and you should have some breakfast."

"I'm not very hungry," Lucy said. "I don't think I'm ever going to be able to eat again. Certainly not oatmeal. Although I might be able to manage a small piece of cake or a chocolate chip cookie, I think."

"Let's see what we can find, then," Chloe said. "I'm a big believer in cake for breakfast too."

"Are you sure this isn't my fault?" Lucy asked as they walked downstairs. "I've thought some really dreadful things."

"Quite sure," Chloe replied, giving Lucy's hand a squeeze.

Lucy wished she could believe her. She wanted to with all her heart. But whatever Chloe said, she still felt certain she was somehow responsible.

27

ARE YOU OKAY, LUCY?" ELLA WHISPERED AS Lucy's classmates huddled around her at recess. "My aunty called this morning, the one that works at the hospital," Ella said. "She saw your mom come in last night." That was the problem with living in a small town. Everyone knew everyone else's business, even if it had nothing to do with them.

Thomas opened his mouth to speak, and Rachel shot him a warning look. "Don't say a word," she snapped. "You are not to say anything."

"I was going to tell Lucy about a friend of my mom's

who had her babies early. And they were fine," Thomas said. "They were completely fine."

The problem was, Lucy didn't believe a word Thomas told her anymore. But she knew he was just trying to be nice, so she gave him a brave smile.

"Have my cookies," Rachel said, handing Lucy a plastic bag with three gingersnaps zipped inside.

"No, thank you. I'm not hungry." Lucy shook her head, fear and worry filling up her belly. She had never felt smaller or more mouselike in her life. "I am not up for eating cookies right now, Rachel. I just need to know my mom and the babies are going to be okay."

"You have to think positively," Rachel told her, giving Lucy a hug. "My dad always says there is a lot of power in positive energy. 'Good juju,' he calls it."

"Juju? What's juju?"

"It's a West African word for 'magic.'"

Maybe Rachel was right, Lucy thought, stuffing her homework folder into her backpack at the end of the day. Maybe she could bring the babies home safely if she practiced a little juju. She needed all the magic she could get. Perhaps some positive thinking would balance out all her bad thoughts from earlier. Or better yet, on her way home she could do five extra super nice things for people she didn't know. If all her wishing that the babies would go away had made them come early, Lucy reasoned, then perhaps she could make sure they were going to be okay by practicing "good juju."

"Do you need help crossing the road?" Lucy said after school, addressing her question to an elderly gentleman with a bag of shopping in each hand. "It's rather icy."

"Oh, how kind, but I'm quite balanced and they're not too heavy," the gentleman replied.

"Honestly," Lucy begged. "I would really like to help. It's much easier to cross the road when you don't have your hands full."

"Very kind of you, but no, thank you," the man said rather firmly, holding his shopping bags close.

Lucy's eyes welled with tears. Practicing good juju was not all that easy.

"Oh, very well," the man said, handing Lucy a plastic bag with a box of tea and a packet of cookies in it. "Perhaps I could do with a little assistance."

"At your service!" Lucy beamed, carrying the tea and cookies across the road. She tripped on the curb and dropped the bag in a slushy pile of dirty snow, and the gentleman scooped it up before Lucy could touch it again. With an irritated sigh he transferred the tea and cookies into his other bag. "Sorry," Lucy said. "That wasn't very helpful of me, was it?"

"I appreciate the thought," the man said, which had to count for something in the good juju department. "Now please, could you leave me alone?"

"Have a nice day," Lucy called after him, just to sprinkle a little more positive energy around. She was starting to feel rather hopeful, especially after catching the leash of a runaway poodle and returning the dog to its owner.

"Oh, you are nice," the poodle lady said. "I was so worried Tami would run into the road."

"Happy to help," Lucy replied, beginning to feel a bit like a superhero.

She held the door of a bakery open for a woman in a wheelchair and then stood there like a door monitor, shivering from the cold, while five more people walked in. As she passed a bus stop Lucy smiled at a tired-looking mother with a wiggly baby in her arms who looked remarkably like the Toad, and judging from the smell, needed its diaper changed too. "What a beautiful baby," Lucy gushed, pulling a funny face and making the baby giggle. "I just love babies more than anything else in the whole world," Lucy fibbed, wishing she were the sort of girl that did. "They are adorable."

"Well, aren't you nice," the woman said, giving a worn-out smile.

When Lucy got to the corner of her street, she stood for a moment, not wanting to turn and see if their car was parked out front. If it wasn't there, she didn't know what she would do. It had been hours and hours since her mom went off to the hospital. Her parents had to be home by now. They just had to be.

The O'Briens' minivan pulled up alongside her, and Mrs. O'Brien stuck her head out. "How are you doing, Lucy?" she asked, looking all motherly and kind. "I saw Chloe this morning, and it sounds like she's taking great care of you."

"Just till my mom gets home," Lucy said, glancing through the back window. She could see Billy staring at his book, turning the pages and chattering away, while Toady (who seemed to have acquired Billy's sucking habit) was chewing on Sammy's stuffed bat. "In fact she's probably home right now," Lucy added hopefully, as the bat came flying past her, landing in the Schniders' front yard.

"You stink bomb," Sammy yelled. "Toady threw Bat out of the window, Mom, and I gave it to him to be nice."

"I'll get it," Lucy offered, grabbing the chance to practice more good juju. She darted over to the Schniders' lawn and picked up the drool covered bat by his soggy chewed up ear. Transferring her grasp to a less soggy wing, Lucy, with a grimace, dropped him back in the car.

"You'll turn into green goo," Micky announced, peering out at Lucy.

"I don't mind," Lucy said. And she didn't. Not if it meant that her mom and the babies would be okay.

"Tell Chloe I'll bring over a macaroni and cheese later on," Mrs. O'Brien said softly. "And come over if you need anything, Lucy. Anything at all."

If she walked backward and didn't step on any of the lines, then everything would be all right, Lucy told herself after Mrs. O'Brien had driven off. Turning around, she walked slowly backward along the street, being extremely careful not to step on any cracks in the cement. It took a long time, and an as an extra safeguard Lucy closed her eyes and turned three times clockwise, then three times counterclockwise.

When she finally felt brave enough to look, Lucy's spirits plummeted and all her good juju slipped away. The car wasn't there, and now she had to face going inside and getting bad news from Chloe. And Lucy just didn't think she could bear that.

28

ARE YOU PLANNING ON COMING IN?" CHLOE said, opening the front door and calling over to Lucy, who had been sitting propped up against Mrs. Minor's fence for the past twenty minutes. "It's freezing, Lucy."

"No, thank you," Lucy called out, huddled on the damp ground. There had been a January thaw a week ago, but the temperatures had dropped again and the piles of snow that had melted like ice cream were now frozen against the fence. "I'm very comfortable out here."

Chloe opened her mouth to speak, and Lucy hung her head, covering her ears with her mittens. "I don't want to hear what you have to tell me, Chloe. I'm not ready for that sort of news." Suddenly looking up Lucy burst out, "Can we go and visit your dinosaur footprint? I need to know that everything is going to be okay, Chloe, because right now I'm not feeling at all sure that it is."

"That's an excellent idea, but you need a snack first," Chloe said. She disappeared inside, returning with a glass of milk and a cupcake, wearing a long puffy orange jacket that came to her knees. Chloe walked over to Lucy and sat down beside her. The cupcake looked homemade, covered in vanilla frosting with sprinkles on top.

"Now, it probably won't taste anything like your mom's, but I did make these from scratch," Chloe said, balancing the cup and plate on the ground. "Jack gave me this nice easy recipe which they use at the diner. And I'm really proud of myself. I didn't burn them."

"Oh no," Lucy groaned. "You have something awful to tell me. That's why you baked cupcakes, Chloe. It must be terrible news if you made them from scratch and didn't use a box mix." She covered her ears again.

"Lucy," Chloe said, and then in a louder voice, "LUCY."

Lucy shook her head. "I can't hear you."

"Your dad called."

"La la la," Lucy hummed, beginning to cry. "I am not good with bad news."

"Your mom is doing fine," Chloe said, and Lucy dropped her hands from her ears.

"What about the babies?" she whispered, shivering from the cold. "How are they doing?"

"The babies have to stay in the hospital for a little while longer, because they are too small to come home. But," Chloe added quickly, seeing Lucy's lip start to wobble, "they will be just fine. I promise."

Lucy felt as if a hot, heavy weight had been lifted off her chest. She could breathe properly again without her insides hurting. "So there aren't any problems?" Lucy said, sniffing.

"No, the only problem is I'm freezing my tail off out here," Chloe said, and Lucy laughed. "Actually, there was something unexpected," Chloe added. "With one of the babies, I mean." And before she could finish, Lucy burst out dramatically "It has three arms?"

"No, Lucy."

"Two noses? Twelve toes. Which doesn't matter a bit, Chloe, because we will love it just the same."

Chloe clapped her gloved hands together. "Lucy, will you keep quiet and listen for a moment?"

Feeling her appetite return Lucy started to peel the paper off the cupcake, which wasn't easy to do wearing mittens. "I'm sorry, Chloe. I'm just preparing myself for the worst," Lucy said. "That way whatever it is won't seem nearly as bad when you tell me."

"One of the babies," Chloe said, smiling. "One of the babies is a boy."

"You mean it has a . . . ?" Lucy couldn't finish. She spluttered out cake crumbs. "That is just not possible. I was there at the scan. There were no little boy bits in sight."

"Well, those scans are not always accurate, Lucy. That's what your father told me on the telephone. Apparently, the little boy bit was hiding between his legs."

"I knew it!" Lucy said, taking another bite of cake. "I definitely saw something wiggling on the scan, but no one believed me." She licked vanilla frosting off her fingers and gave a contented sigh. "This is delicious, Chloe. You are definitely improving."

"I still need to work on my spaghetti though, right?"

"Cakes are far more important than spaghetti," Lucy said, a mellow feeling of happiness spreading through her, as smooth and satisfying as the frosting. She looked at Chloe crouched beside her, pink hair poking out of a red woolly hat, and Lucy couldn't believe she had ever thought Chloe was anything but wonderful.

"Hey," someone yelled, and turning around Lucy saw Mrs. Minor leaning out of an upstairs window. "I know you're both over there. You're leaning against my fence, aren't you? You'll break it."

"It's a fence," Chloe shouted back, but the girls scrambled to their feet and moved away.

Mrs. Minor gave a curt nod and slammed the window shut.

"I mean, seriously!" Chloe grinned at Lucy. "It's a fence!"

"I used to think she was a witch," Lucy whispered, brushing snow off her jacket, "because she was so mean. But now I agree with Rachel, and I think she's lonely. No one comes to visit her, and she hardly ever goes out. That's what makes her so grumpy."

"Well, putting up a fence doesn't help," Chloe remarked.

"But it will be great for the twins to plant magic beans up against when they get bigger," Lucy said.

"Yeah." Chloe grinned. "It's a pretty cool beanstalk-growing fence. I'll give you that."

"You know, we would never have become friends if it wasn't for that fence," Lucy said as Chloe picked up the empty plate and glass. "I'm becoming quite fond of it."

"That's the thing," Chloe said. "You can't change what life throws at you, you just . . ."

"I know," Lucy finished for her. "You just have to make the best of it!"

"Hey, Lucy, do you mind if we warm up first before going down to the river?" Chloe said, blowing on her gloved hands. "I'm just so cold."

"I don't mind at all," Lucy said. "Your dinosaur footprint isn't going anywhere."

The house felt warm and comforting, and Lucy slid off her jacket and gloves, leaving them in a damp heap on the hallway floor. Chloe didn't mind about things like that, which made her an excellent babysitter, in Lucy's opinion.

"I've just had a really great idea, Chloe," Lucy said, following Chloe into the kitchen. She had a feeling she should probably run her "really great" idea past her parents first, but it was bursting to get out, and Lucy couldn't believe they would mind.

"I think you should be a godmother to the babies, Chloe. All babies need fairy godmothers, and I know you would be an excellent one. Aunty Karen is my godmother. She gives wonderful presents and never forgets my birthday or Christmas, and I think you would be perfect for the twins. You could bake them delicious cakes and make them wonderful elf outfits when they get older. And when they're sad and worried about their futures, you could show them the dinosaur footprint and explain that everything will probably be okay." A wide smile spread across Lucy's face. "Which it is, Chloe. I'm just realizing that. You would be the world's best godmother."

"Well, that's up to your parents, Lucy," Chloe said,

looking pleased but a little uncomfortable. "They probably have someone picked out already."

"I don't think they do, and I'm certain they'll agree with me," Lucy said with confidence. But now that she'd spoken her idea out loud, she wasn't quite so sure about this. Maybe her parents would think pink hair, nose rings, and elephant tattoos weren't suitable things for godmothers to have.

29

GODMOTHER?" MR. CASTOR SAID THOUGHT-
fully, putting the key to the grandfather clock back
on top of its case. Lucy and her dad were winding all the
clocks in the house, trying to synchronize the different
times before Mrs. Castor came home from the hospital. The
babies would have to be in a while longer, because they
were still too small to leave.

"She took very good care of me while you were gone,"
Lucy said. "And I think she'd be an excellent godmother.
Besides, we all love Chloe, don't we?"

There was a rather long pause. "Well, let's talk to your
mother about it, shall we? See what she says. But I'd like to

wait a few days if you don't mind, Lucy. She has enough to think about right now with the babies."

"I might have mentioned the idea to Chloe already," Lucy confessed. "Just in passing," she added. "You know how these things can slip out."

"Ahhhh," Mr. Castor nodded. "Ahhhhhhh," he said again.

"I shouldn't have done that, should I?" Lucy said, beginning to sound a bit frantic. "I know what you're thinking. It's up to you and Mom to decide, and you don't know if you want the twins' godmother to have tattoos and pierced eyebrows and pink hair."

Mr. Castor made the sort of throat clearing noise that could be interpreted many ways.

"It seemed like a good idea at the time," Lucy whispered. "Now I feel like a stressed out octopus. I want to chew my arms off." Lucy closed her eyes and groaned. "Mom's going to have a fit, isn't she?"

Surprisingly, Mrs. Castor didn't have a fit when Lucy and Mr. Castor mentioned the idea to her. She was lying on the Nest with a cup of tea, having just been sent home from the hospital.

"I think asking Chloe to be godmother is a really lovely idea," Mrs. Castor said. "I'm so grateful to her for looking after you, Lucy. Chloe has been a lifesaver for this family.

I honestly don't know how we would have managed without her. I've been wanting to do something special as a
thank-you, and this is perfect. She'll make a wonderful
godmother."

"She'll certainly make an interesting godmother," Mr.
Castor remarked, and Lucy gave a relieved smile.

Over the next few weeks Mrs. Castor spent most of her
time at the hospital, sitting with the twins and feeding
them, and then after school Mr. Castor, or sometimes Chloe,
would bring Lucy up to visit. She made her mother regular thermos flasks of a special sage potion, because according to *Nature's Magic*, sage leaves steeped in hot water
made an excellent tonic to help people get their strength
back. Especially when combined with a magic spell, Lucy
decided.

There was nothing she could do for the twins though.
So far she had been able to view her brother and sister only
through a little window, because the nurses wouldn't allow
anyone but the parents to hold them. They were worried
about germs, so the twins had to be in a special room with
all the other babies that needed looking after, each one
lying in a little plastic tank, wrapped up like sausages with
tiny caps on their heads.

Lucy had been every day for the past three weeks, but
this was the first day she was finally going to be able to
hold the babies, who were still called "the babies," much

to the nurses' dismay, because the Castors hadn't officially named them yet. Lucy felt it extremely important that she should be able to see the twins close up before giving them their names, and Mr. and Mrs. Castor had agreed with this. Because what if the name didn't fit? Lucy had said, and how would you know that until you studied the baby's face and tried the name on for size? Names were something the twins would have for the rest of their lives, and it was important, Lucy told everyone, that they got them right.

The Castors had been allowed to use a special room for their visit, but first Lucy had to scrub her hands with lots of soap and hot water and put on a hospital gown. The moment had finally come when the babies would meet their big sister face-to-face, and Lucy was feeling all twitchy and nervous as she waited for them to be brought in.

"Here we are, then," one of the nurses said, wheeling a clear plastic bassinet into the room. Another nurse followed, pushing the second baby. Lucy's stomach clenched. This was the part where Ella would be skipping around the room, clapping her hands in ecstasy. But Lucy wasn't Ella, and even though it was now clear the babies were going to be all right, she still didn't feel like skipping. She just wasn't a baby sort of person, and that is all there was to it. Maybe, Lucy tried to tell herself, it would come with time.

"Ready, Lucy?" Mrs. Castor said as the first nurse picked up a baby.

Lucy nodded, not trusting herself to speak. She held out her arms like her mother had shown her, and the nurse slowly and carefully lowered the baby into them.

"Meet your little sister," Mrs. Castor said.

The baby was smaller than one of Ella's dolls, all wrinkled and prunelike with white flaky skin. She had a mottled red face, a squished nose, and her eyes were shut tight. Peering under her cap, Lucy saw tufts of soft black hair, and sticking out from her head were two rather large ears. Her hands reminded Lucy of tiny chicken claws, curled up and skinny with long, shell-shaped nails. She looked just like an ancient old man. And she was, without question, the most beautiful thing Lucy Castor had ever seen.

"Hello," Lucy whispered, feeling an ache in her chest. The baby opened her eyes and stared up at Lucy, and the ache inside Lucy grew bigger, swelling and swelling until she could hardly breathe. "She looks just like an elf princess," Lucy murmured, kissing the baby's nose. "There is nothing Toady about her at all. And I'm so happy, because I don't have to pretend to like her," Lucy said, flooded with relief. "I really, truly do."

"So any ideas for her name?" Mrs. Castor said. "Since you're not all that keen on Elizabeth, and we really have to start calling these babies something other than 'baby.'"

"Petunia," Lucy whispered, breathing in the warm baby

smell of her new sister. "I think we should call her Petunia. Petunia Elizabeth is a lovely name."

"Yes, it is," Mrs. Castor agreed.

"And what about this little guy?" Mr. Castor said, cradling Lucy's brother and sitting down in the chair beside Lucy. He looked identical to Petunia, but Lucy didn't think he would appreciate being named after a flower.

"How about Ginger? We could call him Ginger after my guinea pig? That would be a great honor."

"No," Mr. and Mrs. Castor said together, rather too quickly, Lucy thought.

Lucy mulled on different names for a minute and then said, "I've changed my mind about William. It's quite a nice name, even if it is a bit royal. He definitely looks like a William." She smiled at her new baby brother, who gave the most enormous gummy yawn back.

30

CHLOE FLUSHED AS PINK AS HER HAIR AND said she'd be honored to be the twins' godmother when Lucy and her parents asked her. Chloe had gone with the Castors to visit the babies in the hospital. "Not that I've got much experience with this sort of thing," Chloe said, twisting her rings around her finger.

"Well, there are a few rules," Mr. Castor said, sounding serious but smiling with his eyes. "No taking the twins out for tattoos or nose rings, or buying them bottles of hair dye before their eighteenth birthdays."

"Honestly, Mr. Castor. Do I look like the kind of girl

who would do that?" Chloe replied, smiling back. "I will take great care of my godtwins."

"Of course you will, Chloe," Mrs. Castor said. "They are extremely lucky to have you."

It was another week before the twins were allowed to go home, and when Lucy and her parents left for the hospital to collect them, Lucy was amazed to see that clusters of tiny snowdrops had burst into bloom overnight.

"First sign of spring," Mrs. Castor observed, admiring the white bell-shaped flowers. "Gosh, I've been so busy lately, I didn't even notice the snowdrops coming up."

"Nor did I," Lucy said. "Because I don't think they were, Mom. I think this is some welcome home magic for the twins."

"Very possibly," Mrs. Castor agreed.

All the Castors felt that a celebration tea party was most definitely in order, but since Lucy's mom spent all her time lying in the Nest nursing the babies, Chloe had offered to bake the cake. It took her the entire day before the party to make it, which meant that Lucy and her dad had to do all the cleaning. But it was worth it. The cake looked delicious, if a little lopsided, and Chloe had even managed to pipe WILLIAM and PETUNIA in green and pink icing on the top and sprinkled the whole thing in edible sparkles.

Lucy's grandmother had driven all the way down from Vermont for a few days. She was going to be sharing Lucy's bedroom, which was most exciting, Lucy told her, because they could stay up late and tell ghost stories, and maybe, if they were very lucky, they might even see Lucy's gnome. Aunty Karen had been invited to the party too, of course. As soon as she arrived Lucy took them both upstairs to her room and had them sit on her bed while she read out Clara's letter.

"Gosh, how wonderful," Lucy's gran said. "I'm sure Clara grew up to be very happy because she obviously had parents who loved her very much."

"Here's the nest they sent her," Lucy said, holding it out for them both to see. "Isn't it perfect?"

"Absolutely perfect," Aunty Karen agreed, admiring the three little eggs inside. "Just like your family, Lucy, a nest with three babies in it."

"I didn't think of that," Lucy said, smiling down at the eggs. "That slightly bigger one is me, and those two little ones are Petunia and William."

Lucy showed them the cookie tin she had found the nest in, and her grandmother got very excited, saying she remembered her own mother keeping buttons in a tin just like that.

"Well, I'm keeping magic in this now," Lucy whispered, opening it up and showing them the gnome she had sketched in her notebook, her list of magical signs, the little pile of sparkles, and the scrap of newspaper with "magic" written on it.

"What a special thing to have," Lucy's gran remarked.

"Yes, and when Petunia and William are older, I can teach them all about magic and where to find it," Lucy said. "And show them the picture of my gnome so they'll know what he looks like when this is their room. Which it won't be for a while, because I'm not ready to move up to the attic yet," Lucy added quickly.

She wasn't ready to give up her gnome cupboard either. Luckily, her new room wouldn't be finished for a while. Mr. Castor wanted to build her a secret closet under the eaves, but he had been so busy helping with the babies, he hadn't gotten around to it. Lucy didn't mind though. She wasn't brave enough to sleep all the way up at the top of the house by herself yet anyway. Still, it was a nice feeling knowing her new room would be waiting for her when she was ready.

Lucy had worn her special leaf dress for the party and put a garland of silk flowers on her head. And when she looked at her reflection in the mirror, a splendid elf princess gazed back. Even the babies seemed to sense it was an important day. They had been doing a lot of screaming since coming home from the hospital, and although Lucy didn't want to give them away anymore, their crying could be highly annoying at times. Often at night now,

Lucy had to put a pillow over her head to shut out the noise, and when the babies weren't screaming, they were constantly having their diapers changed or spitting up all over the Nest.

But today William and Petunia were asleep in their wicker baskets (probably because Lucy had sung them Toady's "stop crying" spell) and were wearing the new soft stretchy suits Aunty Karen had bought for them. It was much easier to love the babies when they were asleep. They looked so fragile, small and helpless, like little baby birds. Which gave Lucy an idea.

Since Chloe was done decorating the cake, Lucy asked her if she had any scraps of ribbon lying around that she didn't need. Unlike most grown-ups, instead of finishing the washing up first, Chloe had produced a big bag of colorful remnants, sensing that whatever Lucy wanted them for was far more important than a clean kitchen. So with Chloe's help Lucy had woven the strips of velvet, satin, and lace through Petunia's and William's baskets. Nests were important, Lucy decided, and the twins needed to have their own beautiful nest each.

At Lucy's request Mr. Castor had worn his magical, rather faded, hummingbird shirt, the blue-and-pink-checkered one that had hung outside for weeks, because how could it not be filled with good juju since a hummingbird had nested in the pocket? In fact Lucy was feeling so full of good juju herself that she decided they should ask Mrs. Minor to come to the party.

"Rachel and I think she's lonely," Lucy said to her parents. "That's what makes her so crabby and mean."

"Ahhh, and not because she's a witch?" Mr. Castor inquired.

"Don't be silly, Dad. I haven't thought that in ages."

"Perhaps we could ask her over for tea another day?" Mrs. Castor suggested, but Lucy shook her head.

"We can't all be over here enjoying ourselves and have her sitting in her house feeling miserable. It doesn't seem fair."

"Well, it can't hurt to ask," Mr. Castor agreed, holding out his hand to Lucy. "Come on. Let's go and see if we can persuade her."

They hadn't even got to Mrs. Minor's front door when one of the upstairs windows was pushed open and Mrs. Minor stuck her head out. Her silver gray hair swished forward, as smooth and perfectly cut as her lawn. "Can I help you people?"

"Hi," Lucy said, looking up and smiling. "Hi," she said again, squeezing her father's hand.

"We were hoping you might join us for a cup of tea," Mr. Castor said. "To celebrate our twins coming home."

"I'm about to take a nap," Mrs. Minor replied. "I always

take a nap at this time. And afterward I'm sorting out my Tupperware. Thank you," she added, twisting up her lips and slamming the window shut.

"At least she said 'thank you,'" Mr. Castor remarked as they walked back home. "And I believe that was a smile, which is definitely progress."

"I think it was a sneer," Lucy whispered. "But I'm still glad we asked her." She paused a moment and said, "I'm also quite glad she's not coming. What if she put an evil spell on the twins like the wicked godmother in *Sleeping Beauty*?"

"I thought you didn't believe in witches anymore."

"Well, I've changed my mind," Lucy said.

The O'Briens had been delighted to be asked to the twins' welcome home celebration, although Lucy was more than a little nervous about this. Something always seemed to break or spill or got hurled across the room whenever they visited, and she didn't want it to be William or Petunia. Not at their special party. Luckily, the boys were much more excited by Chloe's cake than the twins, and they hovered around it, breathing on the beautiful frosting and sneaking sprinkles from the plate.

"Please don't touch," Lucy kept saying, wishing they had a playpen to put the boys in, somewhere nice and contained that they couldn't get out of. She wished it even more when Mrs. O'Brien strolled in and said, "Has anyone seen Billy?"

"Is he lost?" Lucy panicked, looking around the kitchen. There were all sorts of dangers in the Castors' house, just waiting for two-year-old Billy: small clock parts he could swallow, steep stairs to fall down, a toilet to fall into . . .

"He'll be hiding somewhere with his book," Mrs. O'Brien said, rather too calmly, Lucy thought. "That's what Billy does."

"He likes small spaces," Sammy offered, not taking his eyes off the cake. Lucy checked under the table and behind the Nest, but he wasn't there. "I'll look upstairs," she said, racing out of the kitchen. A worrying thought had occurred to her. What if Billy had found her nests? What if he was, right this very second, sweeping them off her shelf and pulling them all apart?

Lucy's groan turned to a sigh of relief as she dashed into her bedroom and saw that nothing had been disturbed. All the nests were just as she had left them, and she was about to go and look in the bathroom when she heard a soft rustling coming from her closet. The door was half open, and pulling it all the way back Lucy peered inside. There, sitting on the floor, with a big smile across his face, was Billy O'Brien. "Elf!" Billy said, holding out his book.

"Elf?" Lucy repeated, crouching down beside him. A tingle of excitement shot through her. "Did you see him in here? In my closet?"

Billy laughed, a bubbly, joyous laugh that could mean

only one thing. And then Lucy saw the name of his book. Up until this moment she had never been close enough (or had any desire) to know what the book was that Billy loved so much. But now she did. *The Elf Family*, Lucy read. The picture on the cover showed three little elves with long white beards, and although their shoes weren't gold and sparkly with curly-toed ends, the elves did look remarkably similar to Lucy's gnome.

"Is this what he looked like?" Lucy questioned, quite sure that Billy was talking about her gnome and not his book.

Billy laughed again, tucking *The Elf Family* up his sweater in case Lucy tried to steal it. Flopping onto his back he chanted, "Elf, elf, elf."

Magic buzzed in the air, so ticklish and powerful that Lucy actually sneezed. "You saw him, didn't you?" she whispered. "I knew he was real. You saw my elf in here."

"My elf," Billy said firmly, hugging his chest.

"Both our elf, Billy," Lucy said. She hesitated a moment and then held out her hand. Billy stared up at her, a little warily. "You can come back again," Lucy told him. "In fact, when William and Petunia are older, you can help me teach them all about elves. And Toady, too. You can all go on elf hunts together."

Billy nodded, and keeping one hand firmly pressed against his book to stop it slipping out, he took Lucy's hand with his other. She led him back downstairs, thinking how amazing magic was. How it always seemed to happen when you least expected it.

Lucy shivered with happiness. She would tell her parents and her grandmother later on, after everyone else had gone home. But right now she wanted to keep the magic to herself.

"Oh, Lucy, you are wonderful," Mrs. O'Brien said, bouncing Toady on her lap. "Where did you find him?"

"In my closet," Lucy answered, smiling.

"He loves closets," Mrs. O'Brien said as Sammy shoved a messily wrapped gift at Lucy. The paper was homemade, covered in crayon superheroes.

"I drew the pictures and did all the wrapping," Sammy told her.

"It's just a little something for the twins," Mrs. O'Brien added. "The boys each picked out their favorite book as a present."

"Not our own books," Sammy clarified, in case Lucy hadn't understood. "We bought new ones from the store."

"That's so wonderful! Thank you," Lucy said, taking off the paper and holding up a smart new copy of *The Elf Family*. She grinned at Billy. "I know the twins are going to love this one!"

Lucy's mother had asked Lucy if she wanted to invite a friend to the party, and without even hesitating Lucy had answered "Rachel." There were days when Lucy still missed playing with Ella and laughing at her jokes, but it was the old Ella she missed, and not the new sparkly one. Rachel had worn green tights and a green dress to the party in honor of elf princesses, and when Chloe met her in the hallway, she gave a loud whistle of appreciation and said, "Cool outfit. I love the tights!"

"This is my friend Rachel," Lucy said. She hesitated a moment, then added, "My best friend." It was the first time she had spoken the words out loud, but they felt completely right.

Lucy led Rachel into the living room and carefully picked up one of the twins, making sure none of the O'Brien boys was nearby. "Isn't she beautiful?" Lucy whispered, thinking that change could be a wonderful thing after all. Petunia gave a little squirm and opened her eyes. And even though she was only four weeks old, Lucy swore her baby sister smiled at her. It was the perfect petunia moment. It was magic!

Acknowledgments

Many thanks to my wonderful agent, Ann Tobias, who loved Lucy from the beginning and never ran out of patience, even when it took me forever to get things right.

I am so grateful to Paula Wiseman for showing me that a little bit of magic is always a good thing, and was just the extra sparkle this story needed. I know Lucy would definitely agree!

Thanks to Chloë Foglia for designing the perfect cover, and to Diana Pedott for the beautiful illustration.

Thanks to Jane Gilbert Keith for all her careful reading and feedback and the gorgeous nest books she let me borrow.

Thanks to my sister, Annabelle, and my mom, who read *Lucy* many times without complaining. And to my dad for coming up with the perfect title!

And to Jon, Sebastian, Oliver, Ben, and Juliette—I love you all.